HER BILLIONAIRE COWBOY

CHRISTIAN COWBOY ROMANCE: STEEPLE RIDGE ROMANCE BOOK 1

LIZ ISAACSON

ISBN-13: 978-1-63876-144-0

"But they that wait upon the Lord shall renew their strength; they shall mount up with wings as eagles; they shall run, and not be weary; and they shall walk, and not faint."

Isaiah 40:31

CHAPTER
ONE

"I just can't believe you sold Steeple Ridge." Missy Marino reached for the roll of packing tape, her auburn braid falling over her shoulder as she secured another box.

Jamie sighed but didn't otherwise respond. Missy tucked her thoughts about the sale of the farm into the back of her mind, though they kept escaping. She'd known for a year that Jamie was going to sell the forty-acre horse farm. But that didn't make the reality of it any easier, and with every book she loaded into another box, every plate she wrapped in paper, every trip she made to Jamie's truck with more of her belongings, Missy's blood felt like someone had poured cement into it and it was now hardening in her veins.

With everything loaded and a professional maid service arriving within the hour, Jamie pulled Missy into a tight hug. The same tight, motherly hug Missy had enjoyed since she was a tween, when she'd first come to

Steeple Ridge to learn to ride. She'd experienced this hug after she'd fallen off her horse, after she successfully got her steed to jump the rails, after she'd won championships, and after she'd come in third or fourth.

Jamie Gill had been part of her life for two decades, and Missy's throat tightened so much that she gasped for air. "I'm going to miss you," she said, not even bothering to conceal the wounded tone, the absolute agony.

The older woman released her and cupped Missy's face in her hands. "I wish I could've sold you the farm, the way we always planned."

Missy shook her head, already too emotionally exhausted to think about why that hadn't worked out. But her mind flashed through her brief three-year marriage—and the mountain of debt she had to show for it.

"You'll like the new owner."

Missy made a face. "Some city guy from New York? I doubt it."

"He needs your help." Jamie gave her a smile as she dug in her jacket pocket for her keys. At nearly noon, with the sun overhead, the day was shaping up to be exactly what the weatherman had predicted—the warmest day in April so far. And yet Missy felt chilled all the way to the bone.

"I told him you were indispensable." Jamie pinned her with a stern look. "Don't make a liar out of me in my old age."

An unbidden smile sprang to Missy's face at the

familiar banter. "Go on then. I'll take care of things around here."

Jamie sobered and nodded. "I'm counting on it. I'll call you when I get to Phoenix." She opened the door and climbed into her truck, the engine roaring to life in such a way that made Missy wonder if the old beast would even make it to Arizona. After all, it wasn't just a day trip from Vermont to the Southwest. Jamie was staying with her adult children as she made her way to her new home in Phoenix, where her youngest daughter lived. Missy was happy for her; truly, she was.

Missy lifted her hand in farewell as her boss, mentor, and oldest friend drove away from Steeple Ridge Farm. She turned back to the house. Two stories tall and clapboard white, it had enchanted Missy on first sight. She'd spent many lunches at Jamie's counter and had slept in the basement when the winter weather kept her from getting back to Burlington, a city about twenty-five minutes from Island Park where the farm was located.

She lived only a hop, skip, and jump from Steeple Ridge now, literally down the lane and around the corner, in her own single-story cottage. She and Jamie had painted the house a robin egg blue the previous summer.

Stuffing her emotions down as far as they would go, she rounded the house, which sat on the back end of the farm, away from the public entrance. There were no riding lessons today—Jamie had made sure of that. All Missy needed to do was attend to the thirty-three horses they housed. The farm owned a dozen of their own for lessons and training. The other twenty-one were boarders, but Missy loved each as if it were her own.

With summer almost upon them, she needed to finalize the brochures for their summer camps and the two horse shows Steeple Ridge was hosting that year and schedule the fertilization of the hay fields. Jamie had included her in every operation at Steeple Ridge, and another pang of regret that she hadn't been able to purchase the farm sang through Missy.

Inside the main barn, the office waited, its list of tasks long and overwhelming. Missy bypassed it in favor of the horse stalls in the front, where she opened the door to Diamond King's stall. The tall quarter horse nickered a hello, and Missy ran her hands down his nose, searching for the comfort Diamond had always been able to bring her.

She led him to the wash stall, calling to Fritz, her golden retriever, to come with them. Fritz hobbled in like the old man he was and flopped onto the ground near the door while Missy lashed Diamond to the lines and got the water going. Diamond probably didn't need a bath, but there was something soothing about the methodical way Missy needed to work to get his light, taupe-colored coat glistening to a shine.

His black mane, markings, and tail made him Missy's favorite—and the fact that she'd won in jumping with him last year. With the sale of the farm, Missy wasn't competing this year, though she still had eight kids to see through to the end of the competition season.

With that weighing heavily on her mind, she finished

brushing down Diamond and led him out to the pasture. It was mid-April; there hadn't been a storm in several days, and the ground was snow-free and mostly dry. Missy loved spring in Vermont, and she took an extra few seconds to take a deep breath and find her center.

Behind her in the barn, Fritz barked, but Missy ignored him. The cleaning service had probably arrived. "Go on," she told Diamond. "There's enough grass for lunch." She needed to get inside and feed the rest of the horses, and her own stomach growled for the want of food.

Fritz continued to bark, the sound grating on Missy's already frayed nerves. At ten years old, he didn't normally get all worked up when someone arrived at the farm. His excitement piqued her interest, and she followed the sound of his growls and barks through the barn to the house behind it.

Sure enough, a truck sat there, but it didn't bear the insignia Missy expected. This was not the maid service, and she glanced around the farm, her heart suddenly cantering through her chest. No one could be in the main barn behind her. The back barn sat serenely in the sunshine; the outdoor arena lay empty.

"Fritz!" she called, and the dog stopped barking for a moment. Then he tore around the corner, his golden retriever smile infectious. He skidded to a stop in front of her, barked, and sprinted back the way he'd come. Missy followed him, her steps purposeful as she anticipated meeting the new owner of Steeple Ridge Farm.

She eyed the black behemoth of a truck as she passed

it. She'd need a ladder just to get in that thing, and it would be perpetually dusty in the summertime. Shaking her head and steeling her nerves, she entered the front yard, where Fritz ran in circles around a tall, dark-haired man with more muscles in his body than sand on the seashore.

Missy's step faltered as she drank in the glorious sight before her. She should call off her dog, but she couldn't quite get her voice to work. Was this the new owner of Steeple Ridge? Why hadn't Jamie warned her his good looks would make Missy go stupid?

He stood his ground, keeping his face toward Fritz as the dog barked and barked and ran in a tight circle. His fingers flexed and released, and Missy wondered what had possessed him to wear khaki slacks, brown loafers, and a light-blue dress shirt to a farm.

City slicker, she thought, as a self-satisfied smile formed on her face. She folded her arms as she observed the squareness of his jaw, the way his scruff seemed to have scruff, and the determination in his dark eyes. Determination she could see from thirty feet away, which spoke volumes.

"Fritz!" she called. "Come."

The dog veered toward her at the same time the man did. He didn't seem to be frozen by her good looks—and why would he be? At barely five feet three inches, Missy certainly didn't intimidate or inspire. She always wore her auburn hair in a braid, and almost always covered that with a hat. She owned two dresses and three skirts for church, and everything else in her closet was denim or cotton for working on the farm.

He strode toward her, his height more impressive with every step he took. "Is that your dog?"

"Yes." Missy reached down and scratched Fritz behind the ears. "He didn't know you were coming today."

"Oh, so you give him an itinerary of who's coming and then he doesn't swarm them?"

Missy tipped her head back and laughed. "Swarm?" She scanned him from head to toe, trying not to appreciate his physique so much. "There was one of him. I think, by definition, a swarm is more than one." She stuck out her hand, though she was simultaneously repulsed and intrigued by the thought of touching him. "You must be Tucker Jenkins."

He frowned and put his hand in hers, pumping it twice. A bit hard, in her opinion, but her dog had just swarmed him, so she let it pass. "And you must be Missy Marino."

"At your service."

His eyes sharpened, but he switched his gaze to the house behind her and the land surrounding that. "So this must be it."

"If you're looking for Steeple Ridge Farm, yes, this is it." Something struck her right between the ribs. "Wait. You've never been here before?"

"This would be the first time."

Disbelief snaked through her. "So let me get this

straight. You bought a horse farm in the middle of northern Vermont without even looking at it first?"

Tucker appraised her, his search almost scathing. "There were pictures online."

Missy couldn't help the scoff that burst from her mouth. "Right. Pictures online." She glanced down at Fritz. "You do know there are thirty-three live horses here, don't you?"

He swallowed, the movement visible and absolutely disconcerting. "I didn't know the exact number."

"Sometimes we get up to forty," she said. "That's our maximum capacity."

A tremor ran across his shoulders, possibly from the spring breeze that had kicked up. "Sounds great."

Missy rolled her eyes, but she hid it as she turned back to the farm. "Well, do you want a tour?"

———

TUCKER NEEDED TO FIND HIS JACKET BEFORE THE TOUR. AND maybe his sanity. Honestly, what had he been thinking when he'd bought this place? At least it came with a beautiful stable manager.

He quickly shelved the thought. He hadn't bought Steeple Ridge Farm to find a woman. Hadn't even known it came with a woman until the day he signed the paperwork. Then, the previous owner, Jamie Gill, had said her stable manager was absolutely the best and was part of the deal. It was even in the sales contract that Tucker couldn't replace Missy for the first twelve months he owned the farm.

"So this is the house." Missy indicated the white, two-story building that had first captured his attention as he'd looked at properties online. He'd never lived in a house that didn't share a wall or a floor or a ceiling with another person, and this country house had charmed him from the moment he laid eyes on it.

"Jamie said a cleaning crew would be here today, so you can probably move in tomorrow."

"Oh, I'm not going to live in the house," he said, some of his earlier frustration and embarrassment at being corralled by a dog ebbing away. He opened the back door of his truck and lifted his windbreaker from the seat. After shrugging into it, he relaxed.

Without exhaust fumes, honking cars, and the pressures of running his multi-billion-dollar technology firm, relaxing had become infinitely easier. Which was why he'd bought Steeple Ridge Farm in the first place.

Somewhere to start over, he thought as Missy gaped at him.

"You're not going to live in the house?"

"I bought a place in town." He didn't need to explain himself, not to her.

"You did?" She blinked, her long lashes distracting him. "Why would you buy a place in town when there's a house here?"

Or maybe he did need to explain himself. Maybe everyone in town would ask the same question. "I wanted to live in town," he said. "I knew there was a house here, but I figured I might not want to live on a farm."

She stared at him like he'd just sprouted horns. "Why'd you buy the farm then?"

"I wanted it." He gazed steadily back at her, almost daring her to ask him another question. Something intimate flowed between them, and he found he couldn't look away from the smattering of freckles across her cheekbones, the intensity in her seafoam eyes, the beauty in the lines of her face.

She half coughed, half scoffed and stepped back, breaking the moment between them. He exhaled, not quite sure when he'd started holding his breath.

"Anyway." She indicated the barn on his right. "That's the back barn. There are twenty matted box stalls there, two tack rooms, and some storage areas."

He said, "Mm hm," like he knew what a matted box stall was. He didn't, but he'd brought his laptop, and as soon as he could get on the Internet, he'd figure it out. That was what Tucker Jenkins always did—he figured things out. That's why he'd founded a company while he was still in college that had grown into the second-largest developer of digital apps. It's why his software—a program he'd written and developed from his apartment in New York City—sold almost a billion dollars annually to video game companies, phone conglomerates, and online retailers.

Not your company anymore, Tucker, he told himself. After ten years, a failed marriage, and more stress than any thirty-two-year-old should have to endure, he'd sold everything he'd thought he ever wanted—and bought a farm in rural Vermont.

He was only five or six hours away from the city—he could go back and get his fix of the fast life any time he wanted. His company also had a branch in Montreal, and that was only two hours north of Island Park, his new home in the middle of nowhere. He'd been to Montreal many times and found the town quaint, and charming, and slow.

Slow was what he really wanted. He craved slow. Wanted to wake up when he woke up, maybe ride a horse, get lunch at a diner that served breakfast all day, and drive on roads that frequently got blocked by two trucks that had been going in opposite directions when their drivers stopped to chat.

Of course, Tucker had never ridden a horse before, or driven a truck until last week, or even eaten breakfast in the past five years.

But all that was about to change. He took a deep breath of air scented like grass and sunshine and . . . he glanced at Missy. Flowers. She smelled like flowers and soap. He caught himself gazing at her mere moments before she slid him a look out of the corner of her eye.

"Did you want to see the horses?" she asked, a glint in her light-green eyes. That sparkle said she knew exactly who he was—someone who'd never seen a horse in real life, if he didn't count the police horses he'd glimpsed in Times Square. And he didn't count those.

"Definitely," he said with too much confidence. "You said we have thirty-three right now?"

"We'll start with one," she said. "He's mine. He's a quarter horse mixed with an Appaloosa, and his name is Diamond King."

"Diamond King," Tucker said, finally able to focus on the conversation, the farm, the woman. He needed to leave his past in the past. Needed to find a way to be happy again. As he followed Missy through the barn and out into the open land, he wondered if simply owning a horse farm would be enough.

She stopped and leaned up against a white board fence and called to the beautiful creature grazing a hundred yards away. The horse lifted its head and came plodding toward her. The closer it got, the more Tucker wanted to retreat. After all, the dog now snoozing at Missy's feet had caged him in a corner of the yard in seconds—what would this horse do?

Missy turned and laughed at him. "Come on, City Boy. He won't bite."

Tucker realized he had backed up a few steps, and embarrassment raced through him. "City Boy?" he asked as he rejoined her. He towered a foot taller than her and probably could've snapped her in half with his bare hands. Yet she possessed a quiet strength that interested him—called to him a way nothing had for years.

She nudged him in the chest with her shoulder as she fondled the horse's mane. "Don't worry, Tucker. We'll get you countried right up. Won't we, boy?"

At her playful tone, a spring of desire for Missy began

to bubble in Tucker's chest. He reached out to touch the horse. When the animal didn't rear up and snap at him, he relaxed all the way, maybe for the first time since he'd graduated from high school.

It felt nice. Real nice.

CHAPTER
TWO

Missy worried her bottom lip between her teeth as she swept out the tack room in the main barn. What had she been thinking? Nudging Tucker like they were old pals? Teasing him like he was one of the cowboys she'd grown up with?

He decidedly wasn't. He didn't even own a cowboy hat, or cowboy boots, and the belt buckle on those khaki pants was much too small. A disgrace, really.

Her face heated as she remembered how she'd analyzed every line of his body, the way he filled out his shirt, the length in his legs, the shock of dark hair she wanted to touch.

She shook her head, finished her task in the main barn, and turned when someone called, "Missy!"

Wiping her hands on her jeans, Missy walked toward Jewel Murphy, who held a clipboard in her hand. "We're done inside," Jewel said. "I just need someone to walk through with me and sign off." She smiled, and Missy was glad to see the friend she'd known since she'd moved to Island Park permanently. "Then we'll be finished here."

Tucker had left an hour ago, a fact Missy both liked and disliked. He'd bumbled around the farm while she showed him the office, talked about the summer camps, pulled out the folders of financial information. He hadn't touched much, and he'd said even less. He was so far out of his league it wasn't even funny, and a stab of longing to have Jamie back almost sent Missy to her knees.

"All right," Missy said. "I guess I can do it."

"Jamie said you could." Jewel pulled open the back door and went inside the house, wisps of dark hair that had fallen out of her ponytail blowing around her face. "So, what do you think of the new owner?"

"He's . . . fine." The scent of antiseptic and lilac air freshener hit her full in the face as she entered the house. It didn't smell anything the way it used to—like Jamie's attempts at southwestern cooking—and Missy felt like her life was being erased, one piece at a time.

Jewel giggled, and Missy couldn't help smiling too. "He sure is fine," Jewel said, before pointing out what she and her crew had done in the kitchen, the front room, the bathroom, and the bedrooms on the main level.

With the inspection complete, Missy signed all the paperwork and handed it back to Jewel. "Thanks for coming," she said.

Jewel drew her into a hug. "It was good to see you. You should come into town more often."

Missy waved at the empty walls. "This place keeps me

busy. And it'll be insane for a while until Tucker figures out how to run the place."

Jewel's hazel eyes sparkled. "I heard you weren't too busy to go out with Everett."

Missy's stomach flipped over. "That's . . . we're not going to do that again."

Jewel cocked her head to the side. "No? Everett's a good guy."

Missy sighed. "Yeah, I know he is." And he was. Hardworking. Faithful. Worked at an accounting firm in nearby Burlington, where Missy's family lived. "We're just not compatible."

"You went out with him once."

"Three times, actually," Missy said, moving toward the front door. She couldn't be contained behind these walls anymore. "I don't know, Jewel. He's just not my type."

"Missy." Jewel put her hand on Missy's arm. "You are going to get married again, right?"

"I don't know." Missy's insides swirled, and she cleared her throat. "What about you and Mitchell? Why haven't you guys tied the knot yet?"

"Oh, I'm working on it." Jewel laughed, the sound joyful and carefree, the way Jewel had always been. Missy envied her. Though they were several years apart in age, Jewel had ridden at Steeple Ridge in the first couple of years Missy had been an instructor. Jewel had attended Missy's wedding to Kelton, been there when it ended, let her have her time to put things back together, and now was here pushing her to get dating again.

Missy had tried. Honest, she had. She'd gone out with half a dozen men over the past year, and none of them seemed like a good fit for her. She was beginning to wonder if she'd already used her chance at being a wife and mother.

"Going home after church this weekend?" Jewel asked.

"I always do," Missy said.

"It's supposed to snow all weekend."

Missy frowned and then groaned. "I thought that was over."

"Last big snowstorm of the season," Jewel said. "That's why I asked. You've been complaining about those tires on your truck for months." Jewel hooked her arm through Missy's as they walked toward Jewel's car. "Come over to my place instead. I'll make that wild rice soup you like, and we'll talk about how you can get City Boy Jenkins to ask you out."

A smile tugged at Missy's mouth. "I'm not interested in him." The little white lie slid easily from her lips, but warmth filled her as she remembered the way they'd stared at each other, the tether between them instant and charged. It had surprised her, and scared her, and she certainly wasn't in a place to have her heart get stomped on again. "Besides, he's my boss."

"Boss with benefits." Jewel's eyebrows waggled, and she laughed. "But seriously, I worry about you driving up to Burlington in the snow."

"I'll check the weather. It's still a few days away."

Jewel got in her car. "Okay, see you at church then."

Missy agreed and stuck her hands in her pockets as Jewel backed out onto the country lane that would lead her back to town. The farm sat five miles outside of Island Park, and Missy took a few last moments to enjoy the silence hanging in the air before she told Fritz to "load up," got in her truck, and followed Jewel.

Just outside of town, Missy turned right and headed another half mile down the road. Her cottage was one of five on the outskirts of Island Park, and she loved the little community of neighbors here. She loved the wide open space. Loved her large yard, where Fritz could chase squirrels and rabbits. The way her backyard edged a wooded area that separated this row of homes from the ones facing the town.

She popped in a frozen pizza for dinner and took a few minutes to put together a green salad, her thoughts revolving through the past three years of her life. From the moment she'd decided to file for divorce from Kelton, everything had turned upside down.

"Not true," she muttered as she cored a tomato. Her life had been shaken to its foundations the day she started dating Kelton Hamilton. She knew that now, though she didn't until the day she'd married him.

After their honeymoon, Kelton had turned into a different person. Different than she'd known in high school. Different than the man who'd hung out on the farm with her, who'd rode through the woods with her, who'd doted on her throughout their courtship.

But after that, every hour she spent at the farm was one too many. Every time she didn't have dinner waiting for him when he got home from work turned into a verbal attack that would take her weeks to erase from her mind. She began to adjust everything in her life, put things she liked on the back burner in favor of activities Kelton wanted to do. She'd started anticipating his mood before he got home, fixing everything she could to make him happy. But none of it seemed to help. Kelton was never happy, and eventually, Missy realized she could never make him happy.

She also realized she wasn't happy, and she couldn't imagine living the rest of her life with a man she didn't even like anymore. So she'd filed for divorce, and if she hadn't trained horses with one of Island Park's police officers, she felt sure Kelton's departure would've been much more violent.

He lived in Montpelier now, where his parents had moved, and Missy was glad she could go visit her family in Burlington without any chance of running into him. The restraining order against him was still in place, and she'd assumed all the debt he'd racked up in her name despite her efforts to talk to the credit card companies.

She'd gone to counseling in Burlington every week for a year before buying the cottage and making Island Park her permanent home. After she ate and with the TV on low, she fell asleep, happier than she'd ever been with Kelton, but still as lonely as ever.

The next morning, she used the public entrance to Steeple Ridge Farm and found Tucker's hulking truck in the dirt parking lot. A flash of annoyance shot through her even as admiration drowned it. At least he was here, even if he had no idea what to do with himself, as evidenced by the fact that he was still sitting in his monstrous vehicle.

Missy got out and lifted her hand in a wave, surprised by how much she liked seeing him there. She'd been determined to dislike him, but she hadn't counted on his rugged good looks or the charming smile he flashed as he leapt down from his truck.

"Morning." He reached back into the cab of his truck and reappeared with two to-go mugs of coffee in his hands. "I didn't know what you liked, but you looked like you'd at least like cream and sugar." He extended one of the cups toward her before he realized she had one already.

She lifted it a couple of inches. "Caramel latte." She grinned. "At least you went to The Bean. That's the best place in town."

"It's the only place in town." Tucker chuckled as he lifted his coffee to his lips.

"That's not true. Harry makes coffee and so does the pancake house. And there's the doughnut shop. They have coffee too."

Tucker met her eyes, a gleam in his. "I like the simplicity of only one coffee shop."

She squinted, trying to put the pieces of him together. Today, he wore a black leather jacket over a white collared shirt and charcoal slacks. His shoes were so shiny, the morning sun glinted off the toes.

"Where did you used to live?" she asked.

"New York City."

She shouldn't have felt surprise, but a vein of it still squirmed through her. "And you came to Island Park? Why?"

"I bought a horse farm here," he said simply. "So." He exhaled, the question-and-answer period obviously over. "What's the first thing we do around here?" He scanned the farm before his gaze wandered back to hers.

"We feed the horses," she said, stepping toward the front office. "We'll have to do some paperwork after that, and this afternoon there are a couple of people coming for riding lessons. Then there are a few kids that take lessons after school."

He blinked at her, his pale, city face seeming to get whiter by the moment. He coughed and took a large swig of coffee. "Can I shadow you?" he asked.

A sigh heaved through her, but she managed to keep it silent. "Sure. Which do you want to learn how to do first?"

"I might lose my mind if I have to do paperwork." He chuckled and ran his fingers through his thick hair. He flinched the tiniest bit before a mask slid into place. "I mean, of course I know how to do paperwork. I just don't want to start my day with that."

Missy smiled. Something about his nervousness was endearing to her. "I never want to start my day with paperwork either." She turned, a flirtatious look in her eye. "The horses then."

———

RELIEF WOUND THROUGH TUCKER, ALONG WITH A HEALTHY helping of desire he couldn't quite understand. His friend and business partner had urged him to get back into the dating pool after his divorce, but the water was cold in New York City, and choppy, and sometimes infested with sharks.

He'd steered clear for years, but now, he thought perhaps small-town life really did hold something he couldn't find in the city. He'd always suspected it did, and as he followed Missy into the main barn, the allure of the slower country life suddenly got a lot sweeter.

She flipped on lights, though natural daylight flooded in from both ends of the barn. She clucked at the horses as she unlatched the barred top of each box stall. Tucker copied Missy by unlocking the bars on the other side of the aisle. Horses clopped forward and hung their heads over the lower part of the stall.

"What are their names?" he asked.

She tapped a black box next to the stall she'd just unlocked. "We write their names here."

Tucker glanced at the black horse that had just lifted its nose over the railing, then to the chalkboard square next to its head. "Cocoa." He'd raised his arm six inches when Missy clamped her fingers around it. A streak of heat shot into the back of his throat.

"Cocoa doesn't like men," Missy said quickly. "I'll handle her." She nodded down the row. "You keep on unlocking the stalls. We'll take this lot outside this morning to the pasture and switch them out with the back barn tenants this afternoon."

Tucker took a deep breath of the air perfumed by Missy's near presence, stared at the spot where her fingers still gripped his arm, and lifted his eyes back to hers. A perfect storm swirled within their depths, and she released him in a jerky movement. "Sorry."

He nodded and moved to the next stall, his nerves buzzing like someone had injected live bees into his bloodstream. He hadn't felt anything like this in a really long time. He'd wondered at one point just before buying the farm if he'd ever be able to feel something for someone again. He had no siblings, and he only saw his cousins every few years. He had his company, a few friends there, his business partner—but no one he really felt anything truly real for.

But as he watched Missy's quick, deft fingers as she put reins on horse after horse and lead them out to the pasture, as she taught him how to harness the horses to the wash stalls and operate the water machinery, and as she led him into the office and showed him who to call to get the fertilizing of the hay fields scheduled, he found he really enjoyed her company.

After lunch, Missy handed him the reins attached to the tallest horse Tucker had ever seen and said, "This is Mint Brownie, and you get to wash him today."

Tucker's insides iced but thawed when she laughed. "It's okay, Tucker. I'll be down to help in a couple of minutes."

"All right," Tucker said, though he couldn't quite get his feet to move. She stepped to the next stall and then the next, slipping the reins around the horses' heads and leading them down the aisle.

Tucker jolted when he realized he'd been staring at Missy as she led the horses outside. As she did everything. The way the horses followed her everywhere—the way that golden retriever wasn't ever more than five feet from her—spoke of her character, her gentle demeanor, her calm spirit.

He ducked his head and said, "C'mon, boy," before taking his first step toward the wash stalls. He had the horse hooked to the lines to keep its head up, and he moved to the sink to start the water. He remembered to give it a few minutes to warm up, remembered to attach the shampoo line before lifting the hose and aiming it at Mint Brownie.

Tucker took a deep breath, unsure if this dark-chocolate creature would take the first spray well. He ran his hand down the horse's back and gave a small pump of the water, the way Missy had. It shot against the cement, and Mint Brownie didn't so much as move.

"Ah, so you're one of the good ones," Tucker said. "Well, let's do this then." He sprayed the horse's flank and set about scrubbing the dirt and hay from the animal's coat. "So how long you been here at Steeple Ridge?" he asked. When the horse didn't answer, Tucker continued. "It's my first day." He moved in front of the horse and looked into its eyes. "How do you think I'm doing? I hope you don't feel bad that you're my first bath."

He glanced over his shoulder but couldn't see Missy.

"I hope I don't mess up too badly," he said, moving around the horse and getting the job done, though the water soaked his shoes and made every step a sloppy mess.

Tucker probably needed to invest in some cowboy boots, a hat, maybe a shirt that didn't have to be buttoned from top to bottom. He hadn't been in Island Park long, but there wasn't much to explore. He'd been to the grocery store last night and found a pizza joint, a couple of places to drive through to get a burger, the coffee stand, and an assortment of shops—including a department store—lining Main Street. Surely he could find something more farm-worthy to wear.

He kept talking to the horse like it cared what he wore, or where he'd come from, or that he thought Missy was the prettiest woman he'd met in a long, long time, concluding with, "That Missy, she runs a tight barn, doesn't she?"

Mint Brownie had no opinion on the matter, and Tucker finished the bath before Missy showed her pretty face again. "Wow, Tucker," she said. "This is great." She ran her hand down the horse's nose. "Not even any left-over suds." She grinned at the horse, flashing those straight, white teeth. "Now you brush him dry." The voice she used with the horse was completely sugar-coated, while the tone she used with him held more power and authority.

Tucker turned back to the shelf above the sink and retrieved the brush. He slicked the water out of the horse's hair as Missy got a brown-and-white horse set up for a bath in the stall next to his. She barely finished before the first rider showed up at the farm. Missy promptly put on a glorious smile and hugged the woman, who was probably five or six years older than Tucker.

Missy stepped back and said, "Tucker, this is Susan DeWitt. She's been riding for about a year."

Tucker smiled, said hello, and shook her hand.

"She rides Mint Brownie. Can you bring him out to the arena?"

"Sure," Tucker said, but he had no idea how to get a horse ready for a riding lesson. Or where the arena was. He figured he could find Missy and Susan easy enough, so he simply turned back to the stable, where he'd put the horse back in his stall after the washing.

Missy sidled up to him and whispered, "Just bring him out, Tucker. I'll get all the equipment from the tack room."

He glanced down at her, and though she didn't linger long, that zing of attraction slipped down his arms and leapt across the small space between them. He blinked, then breathed, and she backed away.

It took every ounce of Tucker's willpower not to turn around and watch her retreat. But he did it. Put one foot in front of the other and collected the horse from its stall. When he made it outside, he realized the arena was inside, so he backtracked and went through the first door just inside the barn. A viewing room sat just to his left, but Susan had come to her lesson alone.

When he passed Mint Brownie to Missy, she said,

"Will you finish with Strawberry and bring her out too? Her rider will be here next."

"Sure," Tucker said, thinking maybe he wouldn't be any good for much more than escorting horses to their lessons. "Which one's Strawberry?" he asked under his breath as Susan set about saddling her horse. He wondered if every horse here was named after a food.

"The one I just washed," she said. "We try to make sure our horses are ready for their riders."

"How often do they get baths?" he asked.

"Every couple of weeks," she said. "Or when they get dirty." She gave him a smile he wanted to catch in his palm, curl his fingers around, and release whenever he needed to know someone on this earth cared about him.

Not that Missy Marino cared about him. He turned away from her and hurried away, confusion coiling through him with the power of a cyclone. He'd expected to be out of his element in Island Park. He'd expected not to know anything, to feel out of place, to have to work ten times harder than he ever had.

He hadn't expected all of that to come with a woman who muddled his mind and stole his breath.

Tucker took a few minutes to stand in the observation room and watch Missy as she turned in the middle of the arena and called instructions to Susan. Susan nodded, adjusted her helmet, and set Mint Brownie to go at the jump again. Missy watched, rotated as the horse moved around the arena, smiled, and yelled more directions.

He hadn't realized what a gem the stable manager would be. He'd assumed she would be crotchety, upset about the sale of the farm, and determined to make his life more difficult. But the truth couldn't be further from that.

Missy simply loved horses, and they loved her.

Tucker turned away from the arena and went to get Strawberry before his mind started wandering to doing something crazy like asking Missy to show him around town. Just maybe they'd end up at the only Italian restaurant in town, or maybe he could walk around the park with her hand in his.

It had been so long since he'd thought about a woman in a romantic way, he didn't quite know how to react, or what to say, or if his feelings were even real. When his marriage had ended five years ago, he'd paid a hefty price, and not just monetarily.

His heart had been shredded, the pieces spread from one side of Manhattan to the other. He held Strawberry's reins loosely in his hands, his dress shoes slipping on a bit of straw on the cement in the aisle, and tipped his head back. "Lord," he prayed. "Help me to understand how I feel."

He didn't expect the earth to shake or a voice to rain down on him from heaven. He did expect the peace that came whenever he turned to the Lord for help. Though he didn't rely on his faith as often as he probably should, Tucker felt assured that his decision to leave the big city in favor of this farm was the right one—and maybe for reasons he wasn't even sure of yet.

CHAPTER
THREE

By the end of the day, Missy's muscles ached, as usual. She'd gotten a lot done, also a regular occurrence. Her mind spun—not normal. She'd been fighting for hours against her natural instinct to flirt shamelessly with Tucker, and it was utterly exhausting.

He met her in the office, where he clapped his hands together in a puff of dust. "So, I need some farming clothes." He hooked his thumb over his shoulder. "Would you mind . . . ? I mean, I don't exactly know what to buy."

She tucked an errant lock of hair behind her ear and pushed away the schedule book. She knew who was coming for lessons tomorrow anyway. "There's not much selection in Island Park," she said. "If you go to Burlington, you'll find a lot more." She reached for her cell phone, which rested on the edge of the desk, her tired mind giving in to the idea of flirting with her new boss. "My family lives there. I could see if they're around. My mom loves to feed people, and I'm sure they'd like to meet the new owner of Steeple Ridge."

Tucker's eyebrows practically disappeared into his hairline, and his dark eyes foamed with amusement. Or fire. Or something. Missy wasn't really sure. She herself wasn't really sure what she'd just suggested.

When it hit her that she'd invited him to dinner with her family—her very large, very loud, very Italian family—her lungs forgot how to breathe. She sucked in air while he settled his weight on his back leg.

"I—why not?" he said, his awkwardness melting into confidence as he grinned. "I'd love to meet some people up here."

Missy forced a laugh out of her too-tight throat. "Well, my family can hardly be counted as 'people.'"

"Oh?" Tucker's voice held interest, and she didn't detect any sarcasm in his posture or expression.

"I have six brothers and sisters," she said. "A truckload of cousins." She stood and headed for the door, bypassing him in the process. She locked up and headed down to the arena, the observation room, the other barn, locking everything up the way she'd done countless times before.

"I don't mind," Tucker said, shadowing her step for step. "They sound fine."

She faced him. "We're Italian," she said, like that would explain everything.

Judging by his expression, which didn't even flinch, her statement didn't explain anything. "Okay," he said. "Should

I drive? Do you want to take your truck back to your place?" He glanced behind him and back to her, then to his shoes. "I need to change my clothes. I'm pretty sure I've lost the outer layer of the skin on my feet because they've been wet since that bath this afternoon." The boyish grin he gave her practically had her swooning. "How about you give me your address, and I'll come pick you up when I'm ready?"

Her brain blanked, so she gave him her address from rote memory and walked next to him as they finished locking up and then headed into the parking lot. Missy's senses didn't return until she'd parked in her driveway and climbed the stairs to her front porch. Then it felt like someone had turned on a giant spotlight and aimed it directly at her.

She spun, sure she'd find Tucker waiting for her, already changed and prepared to drive for twenty-five minutes into Burlington.

"What did you do?" she whispered to herself. It was already five o'clock. With the drive there and back, shopping, and dinner with her family—Missy moaned, the sound carrying through the silent neighborhood—she wouldn't be home until at least nine.

Fritz nudged his nose into her palm, his way of saying, "Hurry up and open the door." She hadn't gotten Tucker's number, his address, anything. So she pushed open the door and let Fritz in, then flew into high gear. If she was bringing a man home for dinner on a weeknight, she couldn't show up with muddy jeans and horse-scented hair.

BY THE TIME TUCKER KNOCKED ON HER FRONT DOOR, MISSY had spent five frantic minutes on the phone with her mom—glad when the conversation had ended with the words "spaghetti and meatballs"—changed her clothes, put on makeup, and curled her hair.

She whipped open the front door, and the step up into her house put her closer to his eye level. "Hey," she said breathlessly, immediately regretting the awed quality of her voice. "You found it okay?"

"I watched you turn off here earlier." He hooked his thumbs into his pants pockets and rocked back on his heels, the hint of that sexy smile she'd seen several times pulling at the corners of his mouth. "Fourth one down." He tapped the door, which matched the color of his polo. "Bright blue door." He grinned; surely he knew the power in his single dimple and beautiful teeth.

"Right." She giggled, and the sound revealed all her nerves. She snatched her purse from the side table and stepped onto the porch, the sandals she wore pinching along her pinky toes. She rarely wore anything but tennis shoes and cowgirl boots, and, well, she was in desperate need of a pedicure and a new bottle of perfume.

Tucker didn't seem to be lacking in the looks-as-good-as-he-smells department, and she took a deep drag of his masculine, crisp scent as she pressed past him and moved down the stairs. She tossed a look over her shoulder. "Did you bring a ladder? I'm not sure I can get in your truck without one."

He scoffed and darted ahead of her to open the passenger door. "I just bought this truck before I moved up here." He glanced into the sky. "I hope it doesn't rain, because I have no idea how to turn on the windshield wipers." He beamed down at her, and she found a range of emotions teeming in his soft yet sharp eyes. She'd been out of the dating scene for a while, but she still had enough wherewithal to recognize the ember of attraction in his gaze.

She cleared the clog in her throat. "So, uh, I just put my foot there?" She glanced at the runner along his truck.

"Oh, uh, yeah." He dropped his hand to hers, his fingers warm and strong, his palm pressing nicely against hers. "Right there." His eyes bounced to hers and back. "Just right there."

She jerked into motion, boosting herself up on the runner and using Tucker's strength to balance herself. "Good thing I'm not wearing a skirt," she joked as she settled onto the seat.

Tucker leaned into the truck. "Do you wear skirts a lot?"

Missy gazed back at him evenly, trying to figure out why he wanted to know. "To church."

His face lit up. "Will you take me on Sunday? I haven't heard anything about when the service starts."

"You go to church?" Missy didn't mean for her voice to sound so shocked.

Tucker blinked. "For a few years now." He double-blinked now, shutters clamping over the emotion in his eyes, closing off something he didn't want her to know quite yet. She couldn't blame him for that. She'd known him for a single day, and she wasn't about to blurt out all her personal secrets.

"Well, church is at ten-thirty on Sundays. There's only one church in town, and it's on the northern edge, by the—"

"Elementary school," they said together. "I know it," he continued. "I live right around the corner."

Missy nodded, noting that he'd bought a second house in the nicest part of Island Park. The man had serious money, and her self-consciousness rose to the top of her skull. He flashed her a brief smile and went around to his side of the truck. While he did, she absorbed its luxury. The leather seats, the glinting silver, the digital display. Just as he got in, a crash of thunder sounded overhead. He froze, his shoulders hunched. Then he started laughing.

"Well, I better get out the owner's manual before we go. I wasn't lying when I said I didn't know how to turn on the wipers."

He reached across the truck and opened the glove box right in front of her. Hers was filled with napkins, odds and ends, and old receipts. His was pristine, the owner's manual the only thing sitting inside.

He muttered to himself as he flipped pages and then said, "Ah, there it is." He bent to examine the lever on the side of his steering wheel and twisted it. The wipers swished up and down. "Bingo."

He seemed so proud of himself, and she cocked one eyebrow.

"This is the first vehicle I've ever owned," he said.

"That can't be true." Missy stared at him, trying to find the tell of a lie.

"I grew up in the city. I can tell you the exact subway line you need to get from Queens to Chinatown. But driving . . ."

Her fingers curled around the armrest on the door instinctively. "Have you driven? You have a driver's license?"

"Yeah, sure," he said, easing a calm smile in her direction as he put the truck in gear.

Missy flashed him a smile and settled into the seat, ready as she'd ever be for almost thirty minutes of awkward conversation, followed by her advising him on what to buy and wear to work on the farm, and then the real kicker: an awkward dinner with her boisterous family—where she'd have to whisper the answers to at least five million questions out of the side of her mouth as she "helped" her mom in the kitchen.

Why had she suggested they go to Burlington? There was a department store right here in Island Park. She could have been home by six, her favorite spinach-mushroom pizza in the oven and her TV on in the background. Fritz would sit at her feet, keeping them warm, and she'd wake up in the middle of the night and stumble into her bedroom, the way she usually did.

A wave of exhaustion hit her, but she stifled the yawn in favor of asking him about his family. When he said, "I'm an only child," horror struck her right between the eyes.

A groan leaked from her mouth, and he cut a glance in her direction. "What?"

"There will be at least eighteen people at dinner tonight," she said. "Plus us." A little thrill traveled from the top of her head down into her toes when she said us. Like they were a couple. Or together. Or anything but mere acquaintances.

He's your boss, she told herself firmly. There's no us, Missy. No us.

"Eighteen, huh?" Rain started to fall, and Missy wished she'd worn closed-toed shoes. "I thought you said you had six brothers and sisters."

"I do. That alone is ten people if we show up. Four of them are married, and I have four nieces and nephews. That right there is eighteen. Mom always feeds a few cousins too, so . . ." She let the words hang there.

"Your parents must have a big house."

"They expanded the kitchen, dining room, and living room a few years ago, when my oldest sister got married." Missy watched the rain lash against her window, and she focused on the individual droplets as she contemplated what the scene would be like at her parents' house.

Chaos. It would be complete chaos. And for someone who had a total of three people in his immediate family . . . A sick feeling settled in Missy's stomach, and she wished she'd brought along a bottle of water to try to wash it away.

"We should just go to dinner somewhere else," she blurted as the idea occurred to her. "It will be super crazy at my house, and—" She bit down on the rest of her sentence, not wanting to admit she felt strange about taking Tucker home only one day after meeting him.

"I don't mind, Missy," he said, his voice low. Husky, almost. Definitely sexy.

She twisted toward him. "You don't?"

"I've always wanted a big family." His fingers flexed on the steering wheel. "I grew up in New York City. I'm used to noise and activity."

"I thought you left the city because of the noise and activity."

"I did."

She cocked her head and studied him, but he kept his attention out the windshield, on the dark road north of Island Park, and she wondered if he was as adept at driving as he claimed to be. He was keeping the truck on the road at least. "Do you like the farm?"

A smile stole across his face, barely there in the dim light emanating from the dashboard in front of him. "I do."

"What did you like the best about what we did today?"

"Working with the horses," he said immediately. He glanced at her. "I wanted to ask you if you'd teach me how to ride."

"Of course," she said automatically, and not only because she believed that the owner of a boarding stable and horse farm should know how to ride a horse. She thought of working so intimately with him and shivers cascaded down her arms. Good thing it was dark on her side of the truck.

"Great. Will we have time to start tomorrow?"

She turned back to her window. "If it's not raining, we can go out in the morning." As silence fell in the truck again, she sent a prayer up that she could make it back home emotionally whole. She begged God that none of her brothers would say anything inappropriate, that her mother wouldn't ask point-blank questions in front of Tucker, that she wouldn't wear her feelings right out on her face for all to see.

As the lights of Burlington came into view, some of her unease drifted away. *Thank you,* she thought, grateful that God always seemed to be there for her right when she needed Him.

————

Missy insisted they go shopping first, warning him that once they stepped through her parents' front door, they might not make it out alive. Her suggestion of going to dinner somewhere else seemed more and more attractive with each warning she issued. Heck, he'd wanted to agree right away, just to spend more time with her alone. At the same time, he wanted to meet her family, see how she fit in, find out if they were as loud and obnoxious as she kept claiming they were.

So, armed with three cowboy hats, six pairs of jeans, two pairs of the best quality cowboy boots he could find, socks and undershirts, and sensible polos and flannel, button-down shirts, he pulled into the driveway Missy indicated.

She didn't get out but stared at the bright squares of light in the house. "What did your mom make for dinner?" he asked, just to have something to say.

"Spaghetti and meatballs." She looked at him. "You're not a vegetarian or anything, are you?"

He shook his head, and their gazes locked together in that electric way that had happened several times that day. His fingers twitched toward her, almost like they could remember touching her and wanted to do it again.

Missy opened the door, effectively breaking the spell between them. "Well, let's go. The sun rises early in the summer, and this night isn't getting any younger."

A smile sang through his soul as he followed a half step behind her toward the porch.

"You ready for this?" she asked.

"Sure," he said easily. Her family couldn't be as intense as she claimed. Plus, he'd been in plenty of high-stress meetings, including lawsuits. He could handle a couple dozen people eating spaghetti and meatballs.

Missy sighed and said, "All right." She knocked at the same time she opened the door, calling, "Mom! We're here."

Tucker waited for her to step up into the house, and when he followed her, a wall of noise hit him square in the face. There really were people everywhere. The two couches in the front room were full, one taken by children who looked to be six or seven years old, all bent over a tablet held by one boy. Their hair ranged in color from blond, to dark brown, to more auburn like Missy's.

"No! No!" one of them yelled just before the entire group shouted and then laughed. A grab-fest began as they started wrestling over who got to play on the tablet next. Tucker blinked at them, unsure of anything at the moment.

On the other couch sat three adults, seemingly unaware of the riot just six feet from them. They yelled over the noise, only adding their voices to it. Tucker glanced away as one of the men made eye contact. He had dark hair like Tucker's, and thick eyebrows over dark eyes that harbored a knowing glint.

In front of Tucker, Missy had continued past the living room toward an open area with more couches, a dining room table, and—as Tucker discovered when he took a few more steps—a kitchen around the corner to the left.

A woman with Missy's light eyes and honey-red hair appeared at the edge of the wall just as he did. An instant smile popped onto her face. "Hello!" She clasped her arms around him and hugged him. Because of his height, he could see Missy as she lifted her arms as if to say, I told you so.

"You must be Missy's mom," he said, grateful he'd been able to force his vocal cords to function.

"Yes, yes." She stepped back. "I'm Lorraine. Tucker, right?"

He nodded, because another eruption from the children would've rendered his words silent anyway.

"Well, come in. Come in." Lorraine ushered him

toward the long counter on the edge of the kitchen where Missy already sat, a hunk of garlic bread in her hand. "Missy," her mom chided as she leaned down and kissed her daughter's cheek.

"What? I'm starving. It's almost seven o'clock. I haven't eaten since noon."

Lorraine turned and grabbed what looked like a metal stick from the counter along the wall where she'd met Tucker. He barely had time to realize what she was doing before the loudest sound he'd ever heard clanged through the house. He actually lifted his hands and covered his ears as she continued banging the triangle. A hum of sound hung in the air when she finally finished.

"Dinnertime," she announced, once everyone had gathered from the four corners of the house, children included. "Missy's brought her new boss, the new owner of Steeple Ridge Farm, Tucker Jenkins. Everyone will be nice to him." Lorraine beamed at him. "And now, Daniel will say grace." She took a step back as a boy of maybe twelve stepped out of the crowd and bowed his head.

Tucker hurried to prepare for the prayer too, something strange and wonderful flowing through him. This is what a family should be like, he thought. Noise and dinners together and an abundance of cousins who liked to play with one another.

The prayer ended while he was still basking in the familial energy in Missy's house, and before he knew it, he'd been swept toward the dinner table by the same man who'd caught his eye in the living room.

"Tucker, huh?" he asked just as Lorraine said, "Leon, let Tucker go through the line first."

"Oh, it's fine—" Tucker started, but he realized that no one else had gotten any food yet.

"Guests first," Lorraine insisted, grabbing his arm and pulling him toward the food on the other side of the counter. "Anthony! Get away from that bread. Guests. First."

Everyone fell into line, and while the noise had dropped several decibels, it was clear that no one would touch a single food item until Tucker did. So he took a plate—not paper. He suspected Lorraine would never allow paper products to be used for family dinner—and scooped a healthy amount of spaghetti onto his plate.

The rich tomato smell that hit him made his stomach tighten with hunger. And the meatballs had a brown crust and put off a delicious, greasy scent. His mouth watered and he took a slice of garlic bread, very aware of the dozens of eyes on him.

Missy followed behind him, somewhat of a buffer between him and the ravenous crowd. "To the table," she said under her breath, and he moved away from the counter to the table. He chose a seat on the end corner, thinking it the safest place. Missy seemed intent on eating as quickly as possible, but when Leon tried to sit on the other side of the corner, Missy said, "Mom's sitting there."

Leon frowned toward the kitchen, and Tucker followed his gaze. Lorraine was busy helping a small child through the line; surely she wouldn't be coming over for at least fifteen minutes. And at the rate Missy was eating, Tucker doubted they'd still be there in fifteen minutes.

"So you're Missy's brother?"

Leon took the seat he'd intended to, and Missy exhaled slowly, making a sound like a balloon leaking air.

"Her oldest brother." He took a plate from a boy who had the same hair as his—wiry and spiky—and set it on the table next to him. "Go get me some punch, all right?"

"Can I have some too?"

"Yeah." Leon looked back at Tucker. "Are you married?"

Beside him, Missy choked. "Leon. Do you think I would've brought him to dinner if he was married?" She met Tucker's eye, a mystery swimming in hers.

"I'm not married," Tucker said, flashing a smile at Missy before returning to his food. He took a bite, and his eyes almost rolled back into his head as the flavor exploded against his tongue. This wasn't sauce that came from a bottle. Oh, no. This was pure Italian love, stewed on the stove for hours. No wonder Missy had been shoveling it in as fast as possible.

"Any kids?" Leon asked next.

Missy slammed her fork on the table. "Leon." She touched Tucker's arm, sending a riot of birds' wings tingling across his skin. "You don't have to answer that."

Tucker chuckled. "It's fine, Missy." He glanced at Leon, who was clearly enjoying himself. "No kids, though my ex-wife did want them."

Leon didn't even flinch. "So you've been married before."

"Once." Tucker liked Leon's directness. He just hadn't been planning to bring up his failed marriage after only one day in Vermont.

Two days, his mind whispered. He'd slept in his Vermont house for two nights now.

"Same as Missy, then," Leon said just as Missy exploded to her feet. Pure fury raced across her face, making her eyes dangerous and deadly.

"Leon." Her chest heaved. "You had no right." She glared at Tucker. "I'll wait in the truck. Did you lock it?"

Was she really going to abandon him? Here, at her parents' house, with the—he scanned the room and did a quick headcount—twenty-one people in her family? And he hadn't even met her father yet.

"I didn't lock it," he finally managed to say. She stomped out, never once looking back. No one seemed to notice her outburst or that she'd left half of her food behind.

Leon shook his head. "She's wound too tight."

Tucker didn't know how to answer, and Lorraine showed up at that moment. "Whose plate is this?" She looked around like she would be able to tell who was missing in this mob.

"Missy's." Leon reached over and slid it toward the center of the table. "There you go, Ma."

Lorraine collapsed into the chair. "Where did Missy go?"

Leon looked at Tucker, who gazed right on back. He

wasn't going to say what had happened; he barely knew what had happened.

"She had to run out to the car for a sec," Leon said. Tucker didn't believe Missy's mother would buy that excuse for more than a heartbeat. She bit into her bread, her frown deepening. After she swallowed, she opened her mouth to say something, but a deafening crash in the kitchen stole her attention. She swept away from the table as people started yelling about watching where they were going and being more careful.

Tucker stared, absorbing the glory of this boisterous family. He grinned from ear to ear at their camaraderie, their blood ties, their pure energy.

He liked them. And even better, he liked Missy. She possessed the same fire—he'd seen it in the determination and precision with which she worked with the horses. The details she paid attention to on the farm. He wondered if her culinary skills matched her mother's, and if he'd be able to somehow invite himself over to her place for dinner to find out.

Only a sliver of surprise pinched in his gut. Sure, he'd only known her a day or so, but she wasn't going anywhere. And neither was he—except, he hoped, back to this house for another family dinner.

By the time he managed to make it out the front door, he'd met Missy's father. A loud, dark-haired man with the same caterpillars-for-eyebrows as Leon, he'd barely paid Tucker any attention. Apparently guests at dinnertime were common fare in the Marino household.

Tucker also carried a Tupperware of spaghetti that

would feed him for a week and half a loaf of garlic bread. He climbed into the truck, where Missy sat stiff as a board, looking at her phone.

He exhaled like he'd just finished a marathon and practically dropped the leftovers on the seat between them. "Wow," he said.

"Don't want to talk about it," Missy said, her voice an even monotone. She'd been waiting for half an hour, and Tucker turned toward her, the words he'd been saving building against the back of his tongue.

"I like them," he started. "They're fun."

She slowly lifted her eyes to his, and even in the dim light he could see her incredulity. "You're joking."

He chuckled and started the truck. "All the kids, the noise, the food. It was fantastic. I'm glad we came."

"You're crazier than I thought."

He laughed now, her seriousness only adding to his humor. "Can't deny that one." After all, who else sold their $25 billion technology firm in favor of running a horse farm? No one Tucker knew, and everyone Tucker knew had tried to talk him out of his decision to leave the big city and escape to small-town life in the middle of Nowhere, Vermont.

But Tucker loved the forests in Vermont. The hills and the lakes. The peace and quiet. The slow pace of life.

She let him drive until they left the lights of Burlington behind. "So," she said. "You've been married?"

His fingers automatically clenched around the steering

wheel, but he forced them to relax. "Yes, I have." He refused to look at her. "You too?"

"Three years," she said. "It's been over for three years."

He couldn't help sneaking a glance at her. "No way," he said. "You must've gotten married when you were eighteen."

Her giggle filled the cab of his truck—and his soul—with a happy sound. "Good one. No, I turned thirty in November."

Tucker full-on turned to stare at her. "Really?"

"Really." She tucked a curl behind her ear. "I shouldn't have reacted that way. Leon just really knows how to push my buttons."

"You didn't want him to tell me you'd been married before."

"No," she said.

"Why not?" He didn't exactly go around broadcasting the news of his divorce either, but he wasn't embarrassed by it. Not the way Missy seemed to be.

"Because it's none of his business. And if I'm being honest, my personal life is none of your business either."

Her words lashed his heart, and it took great effort for him to say, "Of course not," evenly. He wasn't sure he'd quite succeeded, but Missy didn't even glance his way.

"I mean, you're not my boyfriend or anything. Not even close."

He wished she'd stop talking, because a small part of him—okay, maybe not that small a part of him—had considered asking her out to dinner. But he just said, "Right," a tornado of emotions building inside his chest.

"You're my boss, and I'd have preferred to keep the personal and the professional separate."

Tucker pressed his lips together, his brain working on overtime. "Really?"

"Really," she said again.

"Then why did you invite me to dinner at your parents' house?"

"I—" She cut off, her voice there one moment and gone the next.

"Because we didn't have to eat at all," he said. "We didn't have to drive to Burlington tonight. I only did because you invited me."

"You didn't have to come."

Exasperation raced through him. "Missy," he said. "Do you really think I went the last thirty-two years without being able to buy a pair of jeans by myself?"

The dead silence in his truck spoke volumes, and Tucker plucked up his courage to continue. "I knew exactly what I was doing when I asked for your help, which I appreciate, by the way. I probably would have bought the wrong cowboy boots."

She folded her arms and sniffed. "And what, exactly, were you doing when you asked for my help?"

Tucker lifted one shoulder into a shrug, unsure if she was watching him or not. He trained his eyes out the windshield but kept the speedometer ten under the limit, not quite as confident behind the wheel in the dark. "Hoping to spend time with you."

"You spent all day with me."

He almost rolled his eyes. Was she really this dense? "I had a great time tonight," he said. "I hope we can go out together again."

"Go out together?" Her voice pitched toward the ceiling. "What does that mean?"

"It means I'm glad Leon told me about your first marriage. We'll have to talk more about it the next time we go out."

"Next time?"

He couldn't help laughing. Then, employing some of the bravery he'd used to launch his app development company, he reached for her hand and tucked it into his. "Yes, Missy. Next time. I'm interested in getting to know you better—outside the farm. Maybe we can go to dinner together this weekend?"

"Well, I, that's in two days."

"Yes, the weekend is in two days."

She kept her grip on his hand, but she didn't respond. The miles rolled on, and eventually he pulled into her driveway. He put the truck in park and turned to look at her. She was studying their joined hands, her hair falling over her shoulder in a pretty auburn curtain. He longed to thread his fingers through it, smooth it back just before he kissed her.

Don't do it, he coached himself. Don't you dare do it.

He wasn't in New York City anymore, and he didn't think Missy would appreciate his advances if he came on too strong.

"So I guess I'll see you tomorrow?" he asked. "We can still do riding lessons, can't we?"

"Yes," she whispered.

"Great." He withdrew his hand from hers and leapt out of the truck. After he'd gone around to her side and opened her door, she stepped onto the runner and then the ground.

Missy gazed up at him, and though he couldn't imagine a moment better than kissing her under this blanket of stars, he kept his distance.

"Dinner would be great," she said, her lips barely moving.

"Friday or Saturday?"

The corners of her mouth pulled up. "Whichever."

"I'll look at my schedule and we can decide tomorrow. Okay?"

She wove the fingers of both her hands through his, lifted up on her toes, and pressed a kiss to his cheek. "See you in the morning." Then she slipped out of his arms and away from him, like smoke. There one moment—her fresh lemony scent wafting on the air between them, the gentle pressure of her lips against his skin—and then gone the next.

By the time he turned, she'd already reached her front door and pushed it open. She turned back with a smile and a wave and disappeared into her house.

Tucker had no idea what had changed her mind. He didn't much care. She wanted to go out with him again, and his hopes for moving from boss to boyfriend suddenly seemed absolutely attainable.

CHAPTER
FOUR

Missy woke the next morning with Tucker on her mind. And the morning after that. And on Sunday morning too, which really wasn't fair, seeing as how she spent all day with him, couldn't get the smell of him out of her nose when she lay down to sleep at night, and dreamt of him too.

He hadn't held her hand on the farm. Or taken her out to dinner on Friday or Saturday night. It turned out that he actually needed to go back to the city and finish cleaning out his apartment or he'd be charged an astronomical fee.

She suspected he could pay such a fee just fine, but she hadn't said anything. He was supposed to be back in time for church, but part of her hoped he'd run into a wild herd of antelope, or maybe traffic on the freeway between here and New York City.

Neither would actually happen, and Missy stewed over what her friends and neighbors would think of her sitting with him at church. She arrived first and sat in her usual spot near the middle of the congregation. As the minutes ticked by, she thought maybe he had been delayed. She loosened up for a fraction of a second before tensing again.

With only seconds to spare, she heard his voice say, "Just a few more steps, Gladys. I see Missy right there."

She turned to find him escorting Gladys Bright toward her, a huge smile on his face. Missy stood to greet them, automatically reaching for Gladys's hand. "Morning, Gladys."

The woman had to be close to ninety years old, and she didn't get out to church much in the winter. Didn't get out much, period.

Missy slid back onto the bench, and Tucker joined her. Once Gladys was seated on the end, the pastor stood up. Missy didn't have a chance to question Tucker, or even raise her eyebrows in his direction.

Didn't matter. He smelled like fresh air and crisp cologne, and she unconsciously leaned toward him. He slipped his hand into hers and squeezed, causing her heart to ricochet around inside her ribcage. "Gladys is my next-door neighbor," he whispered. "I've been looking out for her since I moved in."

She nodded, but her mind revolved around one thing: she was holding hands with Tucker Jenkins at church.

Giddiness galloped through her the way her horses did when she spurred them in the open pasture, and she knew: she wanted Tucker to be more than her boss.

The thought scared her as much as anything else, and

she didn't hear a single word the pastor said. After the sermon, Tucker said he needed to get Gladys home and that he'd call Missy later. She watched him go, her fingers missing the warmth of his.

Jewel descended not long after that, her questions coming like bullets. Missy tried to dodge them, but her friend wouldn't be deterred. When Missy noticed several other women in town eyeing her, she looped her elbow through Jewel's and towed her outside.

"What's going on with you?" Jewel asked.

"Nothing," Missy said.

"You sat with Tucker."

"So what? He doesn't know anyone else in town."

"He knows Gladys Bright."

"He's her neighbor."

"Do you like him?"

"Sure, he's nice." Missy started to move toward her truck, but Jewel wouldn't be deterred. Finally, Missy said, "Jewel. It's nothing. We work together. He didn't know anyone else. I told him what time the service started, and he sat by me. Big deal," and kept walking.

"It is a big deal!" Jewel called after her.

"No, it's not!" Missy managed to make it to her truck before she smiled. Sitting with Tucker—holding his hand—definitely was a big deal. She'd spent a day stewing over the fact that he'd been married before and that they hadn't talked about it like he'd said they would. She'd tried dating the past twelve months, but no one in town had captured her interest—until now.

As she drove out of the church parking lot, she met a red light and stopped. *Am I ready now, Lord?* she prayed.

A distinct impression came that testified to her that she was ready to move on with her life. That she could actually live a life again. A life she wanted. A life she enjoyed. A life worth having.

———

A WEEK PASSED, THEN TWO. TUCKER DIDN'T TAKE HER TO dinner—at least not one that counted as a date. Stopping to buy oats or pick something up for the farm didn't count as a date, even if they ate a meal afterward.

When she told him as much, he blinked at her. "They don't count?"

"No," she said emphatically. "You can't do farm business and call it a date."

His confusion was cute, really. "And I suppose all this time you've spent teaching me to ride, and showing me how to care for the horses, and revealing your master filing system doesn't count either."

She straightened, the broom she was using to sweep the aisle in the back barn still at her side. "We're at work. None of that counts."

He leaned on his shovel, a mischievous half smile on his face, that delicious beard calling to her to touch. "Well, shoot. Here I thought we were dating."

Missy scoffed. "Holding a woman's hand and buying her pizza doesn't count as dating if you take her shopping for horseshoes and pay the farm bills at the same time."

"I wish I would've known those rules in advance."

She giggled and pushed her broom against the cement. Swish, swish. "Well, now you know." Swish, swish.

"So if I kiss you at work, does that count as a kiss?"

She froze for one, two breaths and then spun toward him. "There is no kissing at work."

"None?" He took a slow step forward, and she scurried behind the broom to use it as a shield, her heart suddenly bobbing in her throat.

She shook her head, but she couldn't get her voice to work. Sure, she'd thought about kissing him. Every eligible woman in Island Park had thought about it. She'd have to be a robot not to have thought about it.

And yes, he'd held her hand on multiple occasions, and they'd worked together in close quarters several times. But now, the devilish glint in his eye spoke of pressing her against the stall wall and kissing her with everything he had.

Truth be told, she wouldn't object.

But if she were playing the honesty game, she was also terrified. She hadn't kissed a man since Kelton, which meant she hadn't kissed anyone but him in seven years.

Seven years.

"I haven't really dated since my divorce," she blurted out.

Tucker's step stalled. "I haven't either."

She appraised him, and she appreciated that he didn't have many barriers in place. She could almost see right into his soul through his eyes, and she marveled at his confidence. "You haven't? You've been divorced for five years." He'd told her about his ex-wife and how they'd married young, how he'd been foolish to believe he could make something work with someone as pessimistic as Tiffany had been.

"Wasn't interested," he said.

"And you are now?" She grinned at him, flirting full force.

"That hurts me," he teased. "You think I go around holding everyone's hand?"

"Yes," she threw back at him. "You hold Gladys's."

He chuckled, the sound dark and rich and wonderful, like her favorite chocolate. "You got me there. She brings me pies and bread too."

"She does what?"

"Oh, did I not tell you that?" He ducked his head so that the brim of his cowboy hat hid his eyes. She couldn't help her growing attraction to him when he did simple things like that. "Chocolate pie and honey wheat bread."

"I think I'm going to need to have a talk with Gladys." Missy giggled, her joy morphing into a squeal when Tucker swept her off her feet and twirled her in a circle. When he righted her and gazed down into her eyes, she thought he'd kiss her despite her rules.

"Please don't talk to Gladys," he said, his voice husky. "There's nothing between us. It's just pie."

Missy tipped her head back and laughed, her hands automatically snaking up to Tucker's neck. "All right," she said. "I won't mention anything to Gladys."

"Good." Tucker stepped back and retrieved his shovel

from where he'd dropped it. "Besides, it's not like I was cheating. Apparently, we haven't even been out once yet."

"True," Missy said.

"So, are you free for dinner tonight?"

"Sure, anytime after six. You should run your errands first."

He growled—a deep, sexy sound from the back of his throat—and she dissolved into laughter again. The sound mixed with the *swish, swish* of the broom as she got back to work.

———

TUCKER DIDN'T KISS MISSY THAT NIGHT. HE WANTED TO, badly. But he didn't. He didn't want their first kiss to happen on their first date. That didn't feel small town to him, and he wanted the small-town experience.

How was he supposed to know that he couldn't mix business with pleasure? In New York, everything was blurred. He had business lunches, and business parties, and he moved seamlessly from work to play and back at all hours of the day or night.

But out here, at least for Missy, things were much more compartmentalized. So he took her to the Pizza Palace, and held her hand as they walked down the street, and asked her questions about horseback riding—and finally, her ex-husband.

She tensed and took a few steps before she seemed to breathe again. "Kelton was . . ." She shook her head. "He wasn't a nice man."

Tucker squeezed her hand and drew her a half step closer to him. "And how did someone as kind as you wind up with an unkind man?"

"He saved his cruelty for after we were married, behind closed doors."

Alarm welled in Tucker's gut. "Did he hurt you?"

"Yes," she whispered. "Only verbally, though. He never hit me."

"Doesn't make it okay."

"Or less hurtful." She held her head high as she walked, and Tucker admired the strength in her. "I went to therapy for a year, but sometimes his words are still there. Still haunting me. Still trying to convince me I'm not worth very much."

Regret raged through Tucker, and he slid his arm around her waist and drew her into his side. "I'm sorry." He pressed a kiss to her forehead, wishing he could've been there to protect her from that pain in her life. "I think you're wonderful."

"You've known me for three weeks." She nudged him with her shoulder.

"I've worked by your side for ten hours a day, seven days a week," he said. "It's almost like, oh I don't know, six months' worth of time."

She didn't agree or argue, and he led her back to his truck. Drove her home. Walked her to her porch, where once again, the blanket of stars overhead created the near-perfect background for a goodnight kiss.

Missy looked up at him with hope and desire burning through her sea glass green eyes. "Well, good night," he said. He drew her into a hug and released her before he lost his resolve and kissed her.

As the weeks passed, he became quite adept atop a horse. He'd chosen a tall black stallion that he owned as his riding horse. Licorice—another food name, Tucker noted—had a gentle demeanor, and Tucker liked learning how to ride.

He could bathe a horse as fast as Missy now, and he could get the farm unlocked and feeding started without help. He knew how to run the farm from behind a desk, but he hated that part of it. So he'd asked Missy to do it, and she said she'd done it before and could keep on with those administrative tasks.

She taught horseback riding lessons and after-school camps. She fed horses and interacted with the patrons as they came to drop off or pick up their animals. It was exhausting work, and Tucker had hired four cowhands to come help with the horses, the planting, and anything and everything on the farm. He'd bought furniture for the two-story house on the property, and the men would bunk there.

By the time June arrived, so had the heat—and the end of Tucker's patience. He wanted to take his relationship with Missy to the next level. He'd been taking her to dinner, and movies, and on walks in the park. He'd hung out at her house, and they'd spent several weekend after-noons with Gladys.

"Let's take the horses into the woods for a picnic," he said one Saturday morning near the middle of the month.

Missy glanced up from the desk, where she was working on something he'd probably hate. "Today?"

"Yes, today." He swept his hand toward the small window behind her. "Have you seen the sky today? It's never this blue in New York City."

She smiled and dropped her eyes back to the paperwork. "I'm sure it is."

"Come on." He crossed the room and sat in front of her. "I've got to get off this farm for a while. Just a couple of hours."

"You have food for a picnic?"

"As a matter of fact, I do." He hadn't left any plans to chance. "And I can saddle my own horse now. I'll do yours too, and then we can go."

"I need to finish this application."

Frustration pooled behind Tucker's words. "Fine. Come find me when you're ready." His cowboy boots made angry punctuation marks on the floor as he walked out. All too soon, hers caught up to him.

"Are you mad?"

"No."

"Yes you are." She tugged on his arm to get him to stop. "That application is for our junior riders. If I don't get it in by Monday, they can't participate in the show."

"That's two days from now."

"We have the new staff coming this afternoon for a meeting, remember?"

"Yeah, that's this afternoon. Plenty of time for lunch in the woods."

She searched his expression, and she must have found

what she was looking for, because she said, "You're right. Let's go."

"Really?"

"Really." She smiled and added, "Race ya to see who can saddle their horse first!" She took off before he could even agree, and he shook his head at her playfulness even as it allowed him to open his heart to her just a little bit more.

An hour later, with trees surrounding them and their horses snacking on grass nearby, Tucker spread a blanket on the ground. He passed Missy a sandwich and placed a bag of chips between them. "Gladys made her famous potato salad." He pulled out the container and two spoons. "It really is magnificent."

Missy giggled, and the sound had wormed its way straight into Tucker's heart over the past several weeks. "Magnificent? Who talks like that?"

"Try the potato salad," he said. "Then you will." He grinned and bit into his ham-and-Swiss sandwich. They ate with a symphony of breezes surrounding them. Tucker enjoyed the silence; it filled his soul to the brim, refreshing and rejuvenating him.

When he finished, he lay down on his back and stared up at the treetops. "I love Vermont," he said. "It's so beautiful here."

"Cities can be beautiful too."

"There's something magical about them, yes," he said. "But there is nothing like this there, not even in Central Park."

"Is that why you moved here?" She'd asked him

several times over the weeks why he'd bought Steeple Ridge Farm, why he'd chosen to come to Island Park. He'd always put her off with some answer about needing to get away from the pressures of city life. While that was true, it wasn't the whole truth, and Missy seemed to know it.

"Sort of," he said. "I'd . . . lost myself in New York City. I was the guy everyone knew, everyone wanted to be, but I looked in the mirror one morning and didn't recognize myself. Didn't know who I was."

She snuggled into his side, and he draped his arm around her shoulder and pulled her closer. With her cheek pressed against his pulse, he said, "I needed to start over. So I sold everything I had and bought Steeple Ridge."

"And a house in town."

He might as well tell her who he was. She needed to know anyway. "Yeah," he said. "And a house in town. And a new truck." He gazed into the sky, stealing strength from the vastness of it. "Missy, I wrote and developed the easiest, most popular interface to create digital apps."

She gave him the courtesy of a few moments of thought. "Was that English?"

He stroked his fingers down her arm to her elbow and back to her shoulder. "That's how I felt most days." He chuckled. "But seriously, if you wanted to build an app for say, your business, or a horse show so people could easily access the schedule, the list of participants, and the outcome, you'd buy a piece of software to help you do that. That way, anyone can build an app without any prior computer science knowledge. Are you with me?"

"I think so."

"Well, I invented and developed that software. It's used in over ninety percent of the apps you use on your phone, your computer, your tablet, everything."

"So you're rich."

He exhaled, the moment drawing into a long pause as he searched his feelings. He trusted Missy. She'd never expressed much interest in his money before, and he couldn't assume she'd care now. But he suspected she would. Most women did, and that was the number one reason he hadn't dated in the city.

"I sold my company for just over twenty-five billion dollars."

She sputtered as she pushed on his chest to lift herself off him. "Billion? With a B?"

He shrugged, which he knew would annoy her. He added a playful smile to the mix when she pressed her lips into a flat line. "It's just money."

"Twenty-five billion dollars." She scanned their surroundings as if a unicorn would appear. She'd probably believe that more than she believed him right now. "So you're a billionaire cowboy."

"Just because I wear the boots and hat doesn't make me a cowboy."

She scoffed and kept eye contact with him. "You work hard on the farm. You know how to do everything now. You're definitely a cowboy."

"Is being a cowboy a good thing?"

Missy's eyes took on a new edge. "I think so."

Desire dove through Tucker. "So we've been out several times now, right?"

"Sure."

"Is this a date?"

She cocked her head to the side, the end of her braid slipping onto her bicep. "I suppose so."

Tucker didn't wait, didn't ask another question. He slid his hand to the back of Missy's head and guided her mouth to his. She kissed him back with as much passion as he felt roaring through his own system. Kissing Missy was like experiencing fireworks for the first time, and as they snapped and popped between them, Tucker deepened their kiss and knew he was ruined for life—no other touch could be this sweet, this superb, this spectacular.

CHAPTER
FIVE

Now that she'd kissed Tucker, Missy couldn't seem to stop. She kissed him, and kissed him, and kissed him, until her lips felt swollen. And still she lay in his arms; the delicious scent of his cologne, the salty taste of his mouth coating hers, and the way his fingers combed through her hair were magical.

He'd taken out the tie and undone the braid in her hair several minutes ago, and it was one of the most sensual things Missy had experienced in a long, long time. She traced her fingertip along the edge of his ear and down into the hair along the back of his neck, a sigh passing through every muscle in her body.

Tucker chuckled, and she settled her face into the hollow of his throat, his strength almost overwhelming her.

"I don't believe you haven't kissed anyone in a while," he whispered. "You're well practiced."

She swatted his chest playfully. "You weren't half bad yourself."

"Half bad?" He shifted, and she lifted herself off his chest to look into his eyes. "I guess I better try again," he said, leaning up to touch his lips to hers once more. Fire raced through her mouth. "I can't be labeled as half bad." He stole her giggle as he kissed her again, and when he pulled away, he was anything but half bad.

By the time she put enough distance between them to get packed up and on her horse, she worried they'd be late for their meeting with the new cowboys.

"It's fine," Tucker said when she mentioned it. "They live right there on the farm. When we get back, we'll talk to them."

She nodded and fell silent, letting the breeze in the birch leaves do all the talking. She tried to avoid hearing him say twenty-five billion dollars, but the words echoed through her mind on a constant loop. The food she'd eaten an hour ago felt like broken bricks in her stomach. She couldn't even look at Tucker. Somehow him being filthy rich made him absolutely unattainable.

And yet, he still seemed to like her. Over the weeks, he'd definitely shown interest in getting to know her better—if him showing up on her doorstep with pizza or bringing her a single pink rose on a random weekday said anything.

Missy definitely liked him, but now that he'd confessed what he used to do in New York, she couldn't imagine telling him about her debts. She'd only told him the basics about her split with Kelton, and she certainly didn't want him to know she hadn't been able to buy the farm she loved because of financial problems.

She thought of her old boss, Jamie, and what she might say. *It's just money, Missy.*

Pretty much exactly what Tucker had said.

Somehow, though, it was more than that.

Missy banished the thoughts about her inadequacy because her bank account didn't have enough zeros by the time they arrived back at the farm. She let Tucker take her horse's reins, and she said, "I'm going to get the office ready for the meeting."

"See you there in a few." Tucker moved with confidence and ease now, two horses trailing him like he'd been a horseman his entire life. Missy marveled at him, at the way everything seemed to come easily to him, at the perfection she'd experienced in his kiss.

Her lips tingled with the memory, and she turned away from him as if someone would be able to tell she'd just had her life changed with a simple kiss. With a heated face, she strode into the office, where she found all four of the men Tucker had hired being guarded by Fritz, who lay in the doorway lest anyone should try to leave before he indicated they could.

"Afternoon, gentlemen," she said as she bent down to scratch Fritz's head. The men wore appropriate farm gear —jeans and boots and lightweight, short-sleeved shirts.

She pointed at a tall man wearing a blue, checkered shirt. "Sam, right?"

He grinned and nodded. "You must be Missy."

She shook his hand, as well as the others'—Logan,

Darren, and Ben—and said, "Tucker will be just a couple more minutes. How are you boys liking the house?" At first, she'd been appalled that Tucker had decided to use Jamie's home as a bunkhouse of sorts for cowboys. But she also saw the wisdom in having someone on-site with the horses, and she could sure use the help around the farm. Maybe then she wouldn't have to work from sunup to sundown.

A former employee and good friend, Holly Gray, was coming back to town also, and she'd be at the farm on Monday to do a checkup on every horse.

"The house is fine, ma'am," Darren said. His hair extended out of the bottom of his cowboy hat, and Missy liked the gentle quality of his voice.

"Do you guys have everything you need?" she asked.

"We went into town this morning," Sam said. "Bought groceries and cleaning supplies." He glanced at the other men. "I think we're all set."

"Boys," Tucker said as he entered the office, though a couple of the cowboys were probably as old as he was.

Everyone turned toward Tucker, and Missy couldn't help the leap her heart took. At least it had happened to an internal organ and no one else had seen it. Tucker gave her a knowing look, though, and she wondered if he somehow knew how strongly he affected her.

She bent her head over the show application for her junior riding team, determined to focus on work at work and personal things during personal time.

She made it through one application before Tucker said, "Missy will take us around. She's the stable manager, which basically means she's your boss. She asks you to do something, you do it. That's how I've survived the past several weeks here on the farm." He beamed at her as he waved for her to go first out of the office.

"Very funny," she said as she approached. "Don't let him fool you. He hasn't survived on the farm."

"I'm still alive," he said, that sexy glint in his dark eyes calling to her very soul.

"True." She stepped past him into the hall. "But we want Steeple Ridge to thrive, not just survive."

———

When Missy pulled into her driveway that evening, another truck already sat there. An instant smile swept across her face, and she jumped from the cab and hurried up the front steps.

Fritz barked and balked at entering the house, but when Holly said, "Come on, Fritz," the dog's tail went berserk, and he launched himself into the living room.

Missy laughed as she hugged her once-best friend, who had moved to Montana to complete a veterinary internship there. "You made good time," she said, once the reunion had ended. "I don't have anything for dinner."

Holly scoffed as she waved her arm, her dark curls bouncing with the movement. "I ate on the way in. I can't resist those apple fritters at Jerome's."

Missy groaned at the mere thought of them. "Who can?"

"I hope you can't, because I brought you one." Holly brandished a box toward Missy, who grinned and took the pastry.

"Thank you, Hols." She sighed, content and happier than she'd been in a really long time. "So, how's the ranch?"

Holly's dark complexion turned waxy, and she couldn't seem to swallow. "I left the ranch."

Missy had been turning toward the kitchen, where she was planning to pour herself a cold glass of milk to go with her apple fritter dinner. Her movement stuttered, but she forced herself to keep going. "You left the ranch? Did you finish your hours already?"

"No."

Missy cast her a look, trying to judge her emotions by her expression, but Holly had always been hard to read. Her Latina fire tended to keep certain feelings under wraps.

"What happened?" Missy asked.

Holly collapsed at the dining room table like the very life had just been stolen from her. "I met an amazing guy."

Missy poured the milk and put the jug back in the fridge. "You seem real happy about that, too."

"I was once engaged to his brother."

Missy's movement did freeze this time, the apple fritter held halfway to her mouth. "I'm sorry. What?"

Holly groaned and buried her face in her hands. A moment later, she straightened and took a deep breath. "I don't want to talk about it right now." She shook her head as if dislodging the thoughts and feelings associated with her time on the ranch in Montana. "Tell me about you."

Missy took a bite of her doughnut and chewed, her mind churning over what she could tell Holly, who'd only been gone for four months. But still, a lot had changed for Missy in the past four weeks, so she opened her mouth and said, "I met an amazing guy too."

Holly blinked at her and then squealed. "Who is it?"

"The new owner at Steeple Ridge. Tucker Jenkins."

"Oooh," Holly teased. "Do you love him?" She tipped her head back and laughed, but Missy actually considered the question. Her gaze wandered to the bulletin board she kept by the fridge—the one where she pinned all her notices, her calendar, her bills.

Cold fear struck her like lightning, and she had a hard time swallowing her milk. "Of course not. We've only known each other for a couple of months."

Holly studied her, a giant smile on her face. "I can tell you like him."

And Missy did like him, so she admitted it. "But . . ."

"But what?" Holly asked.

"He's a multibillionaire."

"Even better," Holly said without missing a beat.

Missy cocked her head and said, "Get real, Holly. It's never been about money for me."

"What? Love? Of course it's not about money." She shrugged. "But money helps."

Money certainly would help Missy, but she didn't want to admit that to anyone—even herself. "I feel . . . inadequate around him now."

"When did you find out?"

"This afternoon, just before he kissed me."

Holly's eyebrows disappeared under her bangs, and her dark eyes sparked with fire. "First kiss?"

Missy sighed and rested her cheek in her palm. "Yeah."

"Sounds like it was amazing." Holly giggled just as someone knocked on the front door. Fritz went wild, barking and leaping against the door once, then twice. He settled into silence immediately after that, so Missy knew whoever stood on the other side had been here before.

She looked at Holly. "Not a word about Tucker or the kiss. Promise me."

Holly crossed her heart and followed Missy into the living room, where they found Jewel standing on the front porch holding a pizza box. "I thought you could use dinner tonight."

Missy welcomed her and asked, "Why did you think that?"

"Saw the four new cowboys in town this morning. Thought you might want to talk about it."

"I'm fine with it. We need the help."

Jewel exchanged a glance with Holly. "Sure, because you handle change so well."

Missy rolled her eyes. "Getting some extra hands on deck isn't a change."

"Dating a cowboy is," Holly said, immediately sucking in a breath afterward. Missy shot a death glare in her direction as Jewel volleyed her gaze between the two of them.

"Dating a cowboy? Already? I thought they were new in town."

"I'm not dating a cowboy," Missy said, the lie sitting heavy against her tongue. She admitted defeat and reached for the rest of her apple fritter. "Fine, I am dating a cowboy, but he's a transplant at best."

"He wears a hat and boots, right?" Holly asked.

Missy nodded, her mouth full of sugar and bread and apples.

Jewel set the pizza box on the table and retrieved a stack of paper plates from Missy's cupboard. "So I'm confused. Who are you dating?"

"Tucker," Holly said, her eyes shining like dark diamonds as she reached to open the pizza box.

"Traitor," Missy mumbled as Jewel's excited yelp filled the kitchen.

———

"GLADYS?" TUCKER CALLED FROM THE ELDERLY WOMAN'S front porch. "You home?"

He heard something on the other side of the door, and it could've been Gladys calling for him to come in. He twisted the knob and entered the house, scanned her front room, glanced down the hall, and found her standing in the kitchen with a carton of ice cream in her hand.

He chuckled. "Eating dessert before dinner?"

Gladys's wrinkles lifted as she smiled at him. With slow, almost painful, movements, she put the ice cream back in the freezer and gestured to the bag he held. "What did you bring me?"

He lunged forward to give her an elbow to hold as he walked her back to her recliner in the front room. "I picked up your favorite sandwich at Harry's."

"You spoil me."

"You gave me three pies last week." He sat on the edge of the couch as she unwrapped the Rueben sandwich and took a bite. "A sandwich is the least I can do."

"You're a sweet boy, Tucker," she said. After only three bites, she wrapped up the sandwich and began rocking. "Anything new between you and Missy?"

"No," Tucker said automatically. "And how do you know about me and Missy?"

"We sit by her at church every week. I've seen you hold the woman's hand. You're not as sly as you think you are."

Tucker's mouth went dry. If Gladys had seen him holding Missy's hand, who else had? And why did he care if they did? He shrugged and grinned. "I like her."

"Mm hm." Gladys leaned her head back against the chair and let her eyes drift closed.

Tucker normally didn't stay long at Gladys's. He dropped by as often as he could, which meant almost every evening after work. He'd learned she had four grown sons, a dozen grandchildren, and even some great-grandchildren. She'd won the best yard award in Island Park for five straight years back in the eighties—a fact she boasted about at least once a week. She had a sweet tooth and liked to bake to support it.

As she asked, "How much do you like her?" he realized she was more observant than he'd given her credit for.

"A lot," he admitted. "Kissed her today."

Gladys nodded, her eyes still closed. "She kiss you back?"

"Sure did." Tucker smiled just thinking about it.

"Don't be so proud of yourself," Gladys said. "You're a big, strong, handsome man. Pride doesn't become you."

"Yes, ma'am," he said automatically, the smile sliding from his face.

"Did she tell you she wanted to buy Steeple Ridge?"

"No," Tucker said, ready to end the visit now. He'd told her about his parents, his job in New York, his favorite foods, and about the new things he learned at the farm. He wasn't prepared for rumors about Missy. "Well, I have to go, Gladys. I'll be by about nine-thirty for church, okay?"

"Mm hm," she said again, and he left her to rock and rock in her chair. Once home, he paced in his house, his own sandwich from Harry's diner forgotten on the counter. He wasn't sure what had his stomach buzzing— the kiss with Missy? The fact that everyone in town might know they were dating? That he'd admitted to her how wealthy he was?

She'd handled that information quite well, he thought, though she did wear a bit of a puzzled look, almost like she didn't believe someone could acquire so much wealth. He didn't really believe it either, to be honest.

"Just lucky," he told himself, finally settling down

enough to open his sandwich. The fact that he'd gotten to kiss Missy was also luck, and Tucker thanked the Lord above for that particular bit of good fortune, wondering for the first time in five years if he could get married again and make it work this time.

He took a slow bite of roast beef and avocado, chewed slowly, and forced himself to think things through. He didn't want to repeat the same mistakes he'd made with Tiffany. Everything about that relationship had been rushed—they met, kissed, and got married in less than three months total.

Tucker would not rush anything this time, as evidenced by the eight weeks it had taken him to kiss Missy. A smile quirked his lips as he thought about the time he'd been able to spend with her, and about the possibility of sharing a lot more of his life with her.

———

ON MONDAY MORNING, TUCKER ARRIVED AT STEEPLE RIDGE first. Well, besides the four cowboys who lived on-site. He puttered around the main barn, scratching the ears of his favorite horses as he unlocked the top half of their stalls. He'd started to lead the horses out to the pasture by the time Missy arrived, and he flung her a smile as their eyes met.

They'd sat together at church yesterday, and Tucker had done a lot more than hold her hand on the bench where no one else could see. She'd snuggled right into his side, and he'd kept his arm around her shoulders for the duration of the sermon. If anyone had been wondering if they were dating, they could stop speculating. Tucker had made sure of that, and Missy hadn't seemed to mind.

"Mornin'," he called to her as she continued into the barn. He wasn't quite sure how to navigate the line between kissing her and working with her. He'd never had an office romance, though he knew lots of his employees had.

She lifted her hand into a wave and disappeared into the main barn. While he'd asked her to attend to the administrative tasks of the farm, she didn't start the day that way. Sure enough, she started bringing out horses, until all thirty-seven of their charges were grazing happily in the huge outdoor pasture.

"I got the boys working on mucking out the stalls." Missy removed her hat and swiped her hand along her forehead, the heat of the late June day unseasonably warm. "After that, two of them will exercise the horses that aren't riding today, and the other two will be out in the fields."

"Sounds great," Tucker said. He knew most of what it took to run the farm by now, but he was glad he didn't have to think about it on a day-to-day basis.

"I'm doing the summer camp this morning, and then I've got practice with the juniors for their show."

Tucker nodded, his fingers twitching toward hers. "We've got eight riders in the show, right?"

Missy finally lifted her eyes to his, and he lost himself in their swirling depths for a moment. He leaned closer, and she seemed to have fallen under the same spell as him, because she let him kiss her.

All the rough edges inside him softened at her acceptance, and he accelerated the kiss beyond sweet to mirror the intense way he felt inside.

Missy drew back and ducked her head with a soft chuckle.

"Sorry," he murmured, not retreating a single inch. His body hummed, the vibrations combining with the energy she emitted. "You're just so irresistible."

Her fingers found his and squeezed. "We do have eight riders in the show, and that's where you come in. I left the paperwork I need you to sign on the desk, and then you said you'd teach me how to build the app for the show."

"I can do that," he said. "I think I know what you want on it."

She released her hold on him and took a couple of steps back toward the barn. "There's a list with the show paperwork in the office. I'm going to go check the equipment for the camp."

He watched her go, admiration flowing through him. Missy had been a true blessing in his life. She'd accepted his presence on the farm without question, and she'd taught him everything she knew free of charge. As she disappeared from his sight, he felt himself falling.

In love? he asked himself, and he found he couldn't quite contradict his feelings. He spun away from the barn, sure he was making another mistake. Another mistake he wouldn't be able to run from this time. Wouldn't be able to bury himself beneath his work. Wouldn't be able to rationalize away.

He tipped his chin toward the sky. "I don't want to hurt her," he whispered. He couldn't imagine doing anything to Missy that would upset her. He saw the weight she carried on her shoulders. She'd explained most of it to him, but he knew there was more.

He got the distinct impression he should go talk to her, so he turned back to the barn and went to find her, knowing that his life wouldn't be the same without her in it.

CHAPTER
SIX

Missy had just sat down at the desk in the office when Tucker's tall frame filled the doorway. Her stomach leapt, and her first inclination was to meet him halfway across the room and kiss him again.

Though she'd told herself that she'd spoken true earlier—there's no kissing at work—she hadn't been able to resist him. And so what if they kissed at work? There wasn't anyone around to chastise her—he was the boss.

When he remained silent, she glanced at him. "What's up?"

"I'm not sure." He walked toward her, his cowboy boots clomping against the pine floor, and sat across from her. "Is everything okay with you?"

"Just fine." She shuffled some papers around on the desk. "Here's the stuff you need."

She knew exactly what was bothering her, but she didn't want to say it. Not out loud. Not in front of Tucker.

So she busied herself with reviewing her lesson plans for that day's camp.

"Missy."

"Hmm?"

"I didn't mean to kiss you at work."

"That's not it."

"I—" Tucker swiped the folder from the desk. "Can you talk to me for a second?"

Missy appreciated the direct way he spoke and didn't want to play games with him, but it still took a great deal of effort for her to meet his gaze. She found kindness and —love?—in his dark eyes, and her breath hitched.

"There's something bothering you, and I'd like to know what." He spoke in a slow, even voice, and the strength in his tone infused her with the confidence she needed.

She hadn't spent much time trying to figure out how to tell him how much debt she had. Every time she thought of it, she distracted herself with something else, frustrated with herself for putting money between them.

"I—" Her voice didn't seem to work; her mind couldn't find the words.

Tucker waited. She hadn't expected a big corporation guy to have patience at all, but Tucker had been nothing but patient. With her. With himself as he learned the ropes of horse boarding and farming.

"My husband left me with thousands of dollars of debt," she blurted. "I—I was supposed to buy this farm when Jamie retired, but it was impossible." Tears sprang to her eyes, where she pushed against them. She couldn't believe it still hurt when she acknowledged that this particular dream of hers was unrealized. That it would never be realized.

Tucker's shoulders drooped, and his face dropped as he studied his hands. "So I show up, with all my money and all my inexperience, and take it from you." He looked at her. "I'm sorry."

Missy sniffled and shrugged one shoulder. "It's not your fault. It's just . . . something I'm dealing with."

His eyes sparked with an emotion Missy couldn't quite categorize, and they held hers for four, five, six heartbeats before she couldn't bear to look at him anymore. He remained silent and still for several more moments—until Missy thought she'd explode if he didn't say or do something. Right at that breaking point, he stood and said, "We all make mistakes, Missy. I've made plenty."

"Sure," she said without looking at him. Of course she knew everyone had made mistakes. Hers just seemed so long-lasting and crippling.

"Thank you for telling me," he said, and left the office.

The fight left Missy's body; her muscles turned soft and spongy. She stared at the empty doorway, wondering if she'd have to pay for her mistake of marrying Kelton for the rest of her life.

"Of course you will," she mumbled to herself. The half dozen bills she had pinned to that bulletin board in her kitchen testified of it.

———

TUCKER WORKED HARD AROUND THE RANCH, ARRIVING before Missy did in the morning and staying after she left. He paid attention to what the other cowboys did, what tasks she gave them, how she interacted with the clients and parents.

He built her an amazing app for the IEA show coming up in the middle of September. He'd shown it to her a couple of times at work, and she'd exclaimed over its ease and professional design; her happiness over having something the other riders and all the parents could use was obvious.

He was reminded why he'd loved his work in New York City. As July faded into August, Tucker felt a pull to go back to the city. But he remembered his life there and how unhappy he'd been. As he leaned against the white fence and gazed toward the forest where he'd first kissed Missy, a keen sense of contentment and joy spread through him.

"You look lost," Missy said as she sidled up beside him.

He lifted his arm over her shoulders. "Not anymore." Without thinking, he leaned down and kissed her, the brims of their cowboy hats knocking together. He swiped his off and kissed her properly, the way she'd been letting him for weeks now. Still, he felt something between them. Something holding her back. But he didn't want to offer to pay off all her debts. He would, but he didn't think she'd appreciate such an offer.

He tucked her into his side and sighed. "So the camps are over."

"Yeah."

"What do you do with all your free time?"

"Advertising," she said. "For our junior teams, and fall lessons, and filling the boarding stalls."

"That reminds me," he said. "I was in the office when the phone rang last night after you'd left."

"Oh?"

"Yeah, some guy named Paul . . . Paul something called. He's got six horses he needs boarding for."

"Paul Fletcher?"

"Sure, that sounds right."

"Tucker," she said, and the crispness of her voice alerted him to her frustration. "Paul Fletcher owns a chain of movie theaters in Burlington. He's one of our biggest clients."

"All right," Tucker said. He was used to working with high-profile clients, and someone who brought them six horses didn't seem that big to him anyway.

"What did you tell him?"

"I said you'd call him back today with our calendar."

Missy spun out of his arms. "And you're just telling me now?" She strode down the path between the two pastures, her back straight and strong.

Tucker hurried to follow her. "It's six horses, Missy. What's the big deal?"

"The big deal, Tucker?" She stopped and glared at him. "He allows us to advertise at all his theaters. For free. He still pays to board his horses here all winter. His daughter participated in our shows, and he donates to the farm."

"He called at six o'clock last night," Tucker said. "It's not even noon."

"You should've told me first thing this morning."

"I could've told you last night when I stopped by. I just forgot. I didn't realize—"

"That's exactly it." Missy jabbed her finger into his chest, and it hurt. "You don't realize. You think because you've shown up here with a bottomless bank account and a cowboy hat that you're a cowboy." She scanned him and definitely found him lacking. Tucker stepped back, his heart breaking into a spasm that peaked when she said, "Well, you're not," and stomped off.

He watched her go, at a loss for what he'd done wrong. Surely this Paul guy wouldn't take his horses somewhere else simply because Missy hadn't called him back at eight o'clock that morning.

He shook his head. No, Missy's outburst was a symptom of something else: Tucker had taken the farm from her.

His heart ached, and the sense of hopelessness driving through him caused him to move to the nearby fence and lean on it for support. How could he fix this?

Diamond King, Missy's horse, approached and nosed Tucker's hand. "Hey, boy," he said to the horse, feeling instant relief simply from the presence of the animal. "Is she always like that? She'll get over it, right?"

Diamond King snuffled, and Tucker took that to mean, *Yes, she's always like that, and yes, she'll get over it.*

CHAPTER
SEVEN

Missy left Steeple Ridge right after she called Paul Fletcher and scheduled his favorite six stalls starting on October first. She'd had it on the calendar to call him on September first, and she'd apologized profusely for not contacting him sooner.

He'd assured her over and over that it was fine. He was simply going to be out of town for most of September and wanted to make sure he had housing for his horses for the winter, as usual. When she'd asked if he needed boarding while he was gone in September, he'd said that he was taking the horses with him to Colorado, to his family's cabin there.

Everything had been fine. Nothing was lost. Missy should go apologize to Tucker for her cruel words, but she didn't have the energy or courage. So lunchtime found her on the road to Burlington, where she hoped her mother would have something stewing on the stove.

As she drove, she realized she was running away from

Tucker. Sort of. "You're really running away from your-self," she said to the empty cab. Everything had changed when he'd kissed her. She'd started falling in love with him then, and those warm, gooey feelings conflicted with the fact that he had more money than a king and she didn't, and that he owned the farm she desperately wanted.

She'd let his money become a wedge between them, growing until she exploded at him over nothing.

Missy pushed her self-deprecating thoughts from her mind. She just needed to talk to her mother, and maybe eat one of her apple pies, and then figure out how to move forward. She pulled into her family's driveway and headed inside.

The scent of baking bread met her nose, further calming her. "Mom!" she called, already knowing she'd find her mom in the kitchen. Sure enough, when she'd walked down the hall and turned the corner, she found her mom standing at the stove with her grandmother.

Even better. Missy smiled at the two of them standing side by side and said, "Is there room for one more?"

"Missy." Her grandmother turned and enveloped Missy into a tight embrace. "Look at you, honey. How are the horses?"

"Just fine, Gramma. What are you guys making?"

"Wild mushroom soup and crusty bread." Her mother took one look at her and startled. "What's wrong?"

"Nothing's wrong, Ma."

Her mom cocked her head. "Liar. What are you doing here, anyway? Shouldn't you be at work?"

"I took today off." Missy stepped away to sit at the counter.

Her mom exchanged a glance with her grandma. "Oh boy. We better get out the strawberry rhubarb jam."

"Ma—" Missy started to protest, but the denial died on her tongue. "Fine. I got in a fight with Tucker over something stupid, and now I feel stupid."

Gramma stirred while Missy's mom bent to check the bread in the oven, the silence they let hang in the air almost suffocating.

"I just . . . he's super rich, did I tell you that?"

"Yes, you did." Her mom pulled a golden loaf of bread out and set it on the granite counter in front of Missy.

"And I guess I'm mad at him for buying the farm when I wanted it so badly."

Her mom nodded, like Missy's feelings were completely normal. She knew they weren't. She hadn't known Tucker before he bought the farm. He hadn't known her. Didn't know of her dreams to own and operate Steeple Ridge. He'd done nothing wrong, and yet Missy felt like she couldn't trust him.

"Is this the man you're dating?" Gramma asked.

Missy groaned and put her head in her arms. "Yes."

"Maybe you should marry him, and then you'd own the farm."

"Gramma," Missy groaned. "That's not how things work."

"Why not?"

"Mom," Missy's mother said gently. "This isn't really about money." She glanced at Missy. "Right, Missy?"

Missy shrugged, but her mother's words set her mind into motion. A sense of belonging and warmth encompassed her as she sipped her soup and talked with her mom and grandma. She spent a wonderful, peaceful afternoon with them before escaping to her old bedroom in the basement.

Her phone rang at six o'clock, like Tucker had programmed an app to call her at that precise time. Still confused, still unsure, she sent the call to voicemail and went upstairs to lose herself among the dozens of loud, laughing Marino family members.

The next morning, Missy met her mom in the kitchen. "Hey, sweetheart." Her mom stirred a pot of oatmeal with vigor. "What are you doing today? Heading back to Steeple Ridge?"

Missy sighed. "Yeah, I guess."

"What have you decided?"

"I don't know."

When her mom stopped stirring and turned to face her with a hard look on her face, Missy braced herself to hear something she probably wouldn't like.

"When are you going to admit you're in love with him?"

"What?" Missy scoffed. "That's . . . that's not what this is at all."

"Mm hm." Her mom brushed Missy's auburn hair out of her face. "You keep lying to yourself, and you'll lose him. You think about that on the way back to the farm."

She turned back to the stove, the conversation clearly over.

Missy didn't stay for breakfast. She gave her mom a kiss, though she felt raw and shredded on the inside from her mom's scathing words, and slipped out the front door before anyone else showed up in the kitchen.

When are you going to admit you're in love with him?

Was she in love with Tucker Jenkins? They had spent countless hours together over the past four months. She'd taught him everything he needed to know to run the farm —and she resented him for it.

"You . . ." She shook her head. She didn't get to blame him for her past. For her financial troubles. For the stark reality that she couldn't afford the farm, and he could.

As the outskirts of Island Park came into view, the first of Missy's tears fell. She pulled over in the parking lot of the elementary school, which next week would be teeming with parents and children but for now sat empty and barren.

The same way Missy felt inside. At least the way she felt inside without Tucker.

She leaned her head against the steering wheel and prayed. Prayed to finally forgive Kelton. Prayed to find a way to release the resentment she harbored toward Tucker. Prayed for help to make the right choices that would allow her to move forward.

She gave herself time to weep, time to think, time to feel. In the end, she pulled herself together and continued toward the farm, where she prayed she'd have the strength and courage to face Tucker and talk everything out.

When she arrived, his giant black truck wasn't in the parking lot. She found Sam and Ben in the main barn, brushing down horses. "Hey," she said, sticking her hands in her front pockets and keeping her cowboy hat pulled down low over her red-rimmed eyes. "You guys seen Tucker?"

"He came in early," Sam said without looking away from his task. "He said he was going down to the city."

Pure fear snaked through her. "New York City?"

"I guess."

Missy spun away from the cowboys, unwilling to let them see her cry. But the tears pushing behind her eyes now weren't from desperation or sadness: they were from anger.

He'd left? At the first sign of trouble, he'd just packed up and gone?

Her fingers trembled as she arrived in the office and collapsed behind the desk. Through her emotional distress, she caught sight of an envelope on the desk with her name scrawled on the front.

Tucker's handwriting.

She picked it up and ripped it open.

Missy,

I'm sorry I upset you over the Paul issue. I can see you got his horses scheduled for the winter. What I don't know is where you went. I suspect your family's house in Burlington, and it's taking everything I have not to drive up there right now. But I respect you, and I don't want to be where I'm not wanted.

Which is why I'm leaving Steeple Ridge for a while. It's obvious you resent me for buying the place, and if there was something I could do to rewind time and prevent your ex-husband from leaving you with too much debt to buy the farm, I think I would. I just want you to be happy.

I tried calling, but you didn't answer. I hope you know how much I've enjoyed my time at Steeple Ridge with you. I'll be in touch.

Tucker

Missy reread the letter, her heart twisting and turning and toppling in her chest. In that moment, she realized that Tucker had become a cowboy: a gentleman with country manners and a good heart.

Not only that, but her mother had spoken true. Missy did love Tucker.

And now he was gone.

Because of her.

———

Tucker exhaled as he stood on the street, waiting for a cab he could signal. The hustle and bustle of the city assaulted him on all sides, and he felt completely out of place in his jeans, cowboy boots, and red polo. Those passing behind him wore black and navy suits, carried briefcases, and spoke into cell phones.

His fingers tightened around his phone, but he talked himself out of calling Missy again. She'd see his call. She'd listen to his message. And when she got back to Steeple Ridge, she'd find his note.

After he'd realized she'd left work early—something he'd never seen her do, or even heard her speak about doing—he knew there was more at play than just him not conveying a message quickly enough.

As he'd stood in the office, a space completely infested with Missy's scent, Missy's touch, Missy's spirit, he'd realized that she resented him for buying Steeple Ridge, for being rich, for being a City Boy in her country town.

He finally flagged down a cab and said, "Central Park at Fifty-Seventh Street." He'd sold his luxury condo in Greenwich, but his parents still lived in the condo they'd bought five years ago overlooking Central Park.

He hadn't exactly told them he was coming. He hadn't exactly planned to take a break from Steeple Ridge until that morning. Well, maybe last night, after he'd called Missy and she hadn't answered.

Tucker reached into the front pocket of the backpack he'd brought with him, his fingers meeting the edges of the papers he'd taken from Missy's house. No one in Island Park ever locked anything, Missy included, and when he'd stopped by last night, he'd gone right in through the front door like he'd been doing all summer long.

She'd left Fritz behind, so he knew she wouldn't be gone long, but the house felt empty and lifeless without her there. He'd let Fritz into the backyard and filled the dog's water bowl, when his eye caught hold of the papers pinned to the bulletin board in her kitchen.

He'd spent a lot of time at her house after work over the past couple of months, but he'd never seen the bulletin board. As he examined it, he realized he was looking at the reason she hadn't been able to buy Steeple Ridge Farm when she'd wanted to.

Without thinking, he'd pulled down all the pages and stuffed them in his back pocket. After he got Fritz back inside, he'd left the same way he'd come, wild ideas flowing through his mind. One of those included him leaving Steeple Ridge, which he'd done that morning.

Leaving the farm had been just as hard as he thought it would be. He'd fallen in love with the quaint atmosphere in Island Park, his little house next door to Gladys, the simple way of life. He'd fallen in love with his life on the farm, the scent of fresh air, the satisfying work of training and riding horses.

He'd fallen in love with Missy Marino.

An invisible weight pushed against his shoulders as he got out of the cab and paid for the ride. As he entered the building and buzzed up to his parent's condo. As he rode the elevator and entered the familiar space.

"Tucker." His mother rose from the leather couch that faced the wall of windows overlooking Central Park. "What are you doing here?" She scanned him from head to toe, her expression filled with concern and curiosity.

He sank onto the couch, though he'd spent most of the day sitting behind the wheel of his truck, which he'd parked on the outskirts of the city. He didn't have the experience with city driving and didn't think it was wise to try now, his emotions as confusing as they were.

"I just needed a break from the farm," he said. "Can I stay here for a few days?"

"Of course." She hurried into the kitchen. "What should I order for dinner?"

"Don't care," Tucker said as he closed his eyes. He'd been ordering in a lot in Island Park too, but he missed Gladys's bread and pies. The thought of trying to fall asleep in the city had Tucker's muscles tight and his mind buzzing. He craved the silence and solitude of Island Park, and he wondered how long he could possibly stay in New York City.

"Chinese is on its way." His mother joined him on the couch. "Trouble on the farm?"

Tucker opened his eyes and took a moment to focus on his mom's face. She'd tried to talk him out of selling his company and moving six hours away from everyone and everything he knew.

"The farm's great," he said, speaking true. "It's . . . It's my girlfriend that's got me unhappy."

His mother's eyebrows shot under her dyed-blonde bangs. "Girlfriend?" She reached over and set her wine glass down on the coffee table, giving him her full attention. "Tucker." A hopeful smile graced her face. "You're dating again?"

Tucker took off his cowboy hat and ran his fingers through his hair. "I was, yeah."

"That's wonderful."

"She's mad at me for buying the farm." A sense of injustice filled him. He'd had no idea she'd wanted to buy the farm. Steeple Ridge had been on the market for six months before he'd found it and bought it. Intellectually, he knew it wasn't his fault, knew he'd done nothing wrong by purchasing Steeple Ridge. But the fact remained that the farm was a huge, engulfing beast between him and Missy, something she couldn't seem to get past.

He exhaled. "I think I'm gonna sell it."

"The farm?"

"Yeah." He got up, unsurprised when his mom scrambled after him. "I'm going to go shower." He tried to give her a smile, but it didn't come off quite right. She let him go, and Tucker stooped for his backpack before sequestering himself in the guest bedroom.

He wasn't sure of the consequences of his actions, and he didn't pause to think through them. He'd done all that already, and he suspected Missy would be downright furious when she found out he'd paid her debts.

He didn't care. If that was what it took for her to be able to buy Steeple Ridge, so be it. An edge of hope crept into his soul as he made the phone calls necessary to erase the problems her ex-husband had left her with. He might be crazy, but well, he already knew that. Who else would buy a horse farm without having actually seen a horse in real life?

With her bills paid, and a call out to his realtor about listing Steeple Ridge for sale, Tucker stepped into the shower, that weight he'd been carrying since last night finally evaporating under the hot water.

———

His phone showed three missed calls by the time he returned to the bedroom. Not only that, but his mother had knocked on the bathroom door twice, first to tell him that the food had arrived and then to say his father had.

Tucker stuck his head into the hall. "Mom, I'll be a few more minutes."

"All right," she said, a heavy note of frustration in her voice. Tucker didn't care. He didn't care, because all three missed calls were from Missy.

Still, he hesitated to call her. She'd be angry he'd paid her bills. But how had she found out already? Maybe she had payment notices set up through her email or text messages.

His heart hammered in the back of his throat. He didn't want her to have another reason to be angry with him. His head felt too heavy to hold up, and he let his chin dip to his chest. He shouldn't have paid her debts.

He finally let his thumb drop onto the call button and lifted the phone to his ear. It rang twice before Missy said, "Tucker," in the coldest voice he'd ever heard.

"Missy," he replied.

"Where are you?"

"New York City."

"Did you come in my house?"

"Yes."

She exhaled and said, "You took my bills." Her voice wavered on the last couple of words, and Tucker wished he were there with her to gather her close and whisper that he loved her, that he'd do anything to make her life easier.

"I did." Sniffling came through the line, and Tucker's world crashed. "Missy, I'm putting Steeple Ridge up for sale. I took your bills so I could pay them, so you could buy the farm."

Only silence answered him, and if it hadn't been for an occasional bark from Fritz in the background, Tucker would've thought she'd hung up.

"I'll let you know when my realtor lists the farm. I'll sell it to you, whatever you offer." He gave her another few seconds to respond, and when she didn't, he added, "Goodbye, Missy," and hung up.

He stared at the squeaky-clean floor, the scent of sweet-and-sour chicken wafting down the hall and into the bedroom. His divorce hadn't felt this heart-wrenching, and he knew why: he hadn't been in love with Tiffany. Everything with her had been a nuisance, a thorn in his side. He'd given her whatever she wanted just to get her out of his life. He hadn't looked back or been particularly heartbroken.

He'd just lost his ability to trust himself, rely on his own instincts. "Until the farm," he murmured. Everyone had called him crazy, advised him not to do it, but it had been the single best thing he'd done in his thirty-two years of life.

Thoughts whirling, he turned off his phone and inhaled new strength into his lungs, his limbs, before heading into the kitchen. "Hey, Dad." He clapped his hand on his father's shoulder. "Things okay in the office?" His father worked as a senior partner in a marketing firm located in one of the tall buildings in Manhattan.

"Good enough." He nudged the ham fried rice toward Tucker. "Saved this for you."

"Narrowly," his mother added with a teasing smile.

"Thanks." Tucker shoveled the rice, some chicken, and a bit of beef onto his plate. He snatched an egg roll and sat next to his father at the long counter dividing the kitchen from the living room.

"How's the farm?" his mother asked.

"I'm selling it," he said. He noticed the concerned glances his parents exchanged. "You were right. It's not for me."

His mom nodded and continued eating. Tucker thought he might get lucky and get through dinner without having to explain much more than that.

"I think it is for you," his father said.

"Oh yeah?" Tucker leaned away from his dad and stabbed a piece of broccoli. "And how would you know?"

His father, though getting up there in years, hadn't lost the edge in his eyes. "Your messages the past few months have seemed happier than you've ever been."

"Yeah, well." Tucker ducked his head and stuffed more food in his mouth. "That doesn't really have anything to do with the farm."

"Right." His dad slid his empty plate into the sink. "So what's her name?" He waved his hand. "This woman you told your mom you were dating?"

Tucker didn't see any reason to deny it. "Missy." He sighed miserably, every cell in his body so, so tired. "It's been a long day," he said. "I'm going to go to bed." It was inconceivable to go to bed at seven-thirty in New York City, but his parents didn't object. He stood at the window and gazed over the city, his eyes flitting from one building to the next, one water tower to the next, watching the traffic stream by below.

He felt as rushed inside, as unsettled, as insignificant. After pulling the curtains closed, he retreated to his laptop, trying to sort through what he could do in Island Park after he sold the farm. Trying to decide if he could even live in such a small town with the woman he loved and not be with her.

CHAPTER
EIGHT

Missy spent the evening in tears, her feet wearing a path in the kitchen floor as she paced back and forth. She couldn't believe Tucker had paid her debts. The sense of relief when he'd told her had been immediate and crippling. It was a true miracle, and she couldn't even articulate how grateful she was.

At the same time, she was absolutely horrified and incredibly furious. Her debts were her problem, not his. He had no right kept streaming through her head, along with, I'm so glad he did.

She couldn't live on this teeter-totter for much longer. She grabbed her keys and whistled at Fritz. "Come on," she said. "Wanna go for a ride?" The dog always did, and he loaded up with his tongue lolling out of his mouth, ready for whatever adventure lay ahead.

Missy wasn't even sure where she was going. She just drove. Drove down Main Street, with its sticky-shoe theater, the barbershop where the men gathered to get their hair cut, the grocery store, the department store, a bakery, and the diner. She turned the corner and slowed as a pair of teenage girls stepped into the street to cross in front of her.

With the sun on the way down, the light glinted off the windows of the post office, a candy shop, the pizza joint where the girls were headed, and several other shops and businesses Missy had visited dozens of times for different reasons.

She loved this town. She had since the moment her mother had first driven her here for her first riding lesson when she was ten years old. She'd always wanted to live in Island Park and work at Steeple Ridge Farm. As she eased her truck forward again, she realized she'd achieved those dreams.

She did live in Island Park, in a cozy home she loved.

She did work at Steeple Ridge Farm, the land she'd loved for two decades.

Stopped at the red light, she had the distinct thought to go visit Gladys Bright. She knew where the woman lived; Gladys might be the oldest resident of Island Park, and everyone knew where she lived.

Missy pulled into the driveway and didn't hesitate to get out of her truck. She glanced next door, to Tucker's house. She'd never come to his place; he always stopped by hers. He'd take Gladys home and then come over on Sunday afternoons. Brought her pizza and flowers and his quick laugh, sexy smile, and welcome company.

She shook her head as she walked up the steps and

rang Gladys's doorbell. Missy knew before she heard Gladys's feeble call to come in that she'd made a mistake with Tucker. A huge mistake, and she needed to fix it, fast, before she lost him forever.

"Gladys," she said when she found the woman in the living room, rocking in an obviously well-loved chair. "How are you?"

"It's been a long day," the woman said.

Missy perched on the couch across from her. "Why's that?"

"Tucker stopped by this morning and said he doesn't need any more pies."

All of Missy's hopes dried up, leaving behind cracks in her soul. "He loves your pies."

"Said he was going back to the city. Wouldn't be back for a few days." She harrumphed. "So I had to eat the apple pie myself, and then I hobbled on down the street to the Ballard's with the cherry one. Did you know a person can be allergic to gluten?" She scoffed and waved a veined hand like she'd been told Bigfoot had been found in her backyard. "Strangest thing I've ever heard."

Missy nodded, but her mind had been stuck on a few days. Tucker was coming back. And she'd make sure the whole town welcomed him when he did.

"Do you like cherry pie?" Gladys asked, and Missy dissolved into giggles.

"I sure do, Gladys."

"Great. There's a pie on the kitchen counter. You can have it."

———

TUCKER DIDN'T COME BACK IN "A FEW DAYS." THE WEEKEND came and went, and he still didn't show up. Missy had recruited everyone she knew to keep a lookout for him, from Harry at the diner, to Jerome at the bakery, to Gladys herself, who claimed she hadn't stopped staring out her front window at Tucker's driveway for four straight days.

By day six, Missy's desperation had grown to epic proportions. She dug her pitchfork into the bedding in Diamond King's stall and heaved it out. Over and over, she strained her muscles, hoping the physical exertion would drive away some of her emotional anguish.

It didn't, but she got the job done.

"Missy," Ben called from the back end of the main barn.

"Yeah?" She arched her back to work out the ache there.

"We've got some trouble in the back barn."

She abandoned her pitchfork and headed down the aisle immediately, no more questions asked. The two barns stood thirty yards apart, and she broke into a run as she exited the main barn.

She saw a couple of cowboys out of the corner of her eye, standing to her left near the outdoor corral. "Ben?" She veered in that direction, her pulse plummeting and then bouncing to the back of her throat.

"Three horses got out," he said, gesturing to the land beyond. Sam and Darren had already gotten lassos and gone out to head off the horses, but Missy felt like she might faint when she saw the animals.

"Those are Paul Fletcher's horses," she said, her voice little more than air.

"Their gates weren't locked after they were brought back in from pasture," Ben said.

"That can't be right," Missy said, trying to remember if she'd set the latches or not. She couldn't remember. So much of her mental energy got spent on thinking about Tucker, waiting for a text or call that someone had seen Tucker, or fantasizing that when she turned around, she'd see Tucker.

"Latches didn't close," Ben said. "I don't know how long they've been out there."

"Well, they haven't run off," Missy said. "I'll go saddle up Diamond."

"Sam and Darren can get them," he said. "I just wanted you to know."

Missy turned, a response almost past her vocal cords when she froze from feet to skull as if she'd been hit with a freeze ray.

"Tucker," she said.

"What's going on?" he asked, barely paying her any attention at all.

"Oh, hey," Ben said. "Couple of Paul's horses got out. We're gettin' 'em rounded up now."

Missy felt like someone had hit her with a bolt of lightning, and as Tucker's delectable scent of sunshine, fresh air, and that spicy cologne infused her senses, she trembled. He spoke, but his voice warbled into a single stream of noise.

She couldn't believe he was here, that no one had seen him first, that he hadn't gone home before coming by the farm.

Then he appeared right in front of her, his fingers sliding down her bare arm to claim her fingers. Still she stared at him, unsure of when her tongue had tied itself into a knot.

"Can I talk to you?" he asked. He didn't wait for her to answer before he released her and moved back into the main barn, seemingly unfazed that they had horses loose or that she'd turned dumb at the mere sight of him.

Somehow, she got her feet to stumble after him, catching sight of him just as he ducked into the office. She joined him, closed the door, and pressed her back against it. "Tucker," she said again. "You came back."

He stood at the desk, looking at something, refusing to meet her gaze. "The farm should be up for sale tomorrow."

His words snapped her back to reality. "I don't care about the farm." Tucker turned toward her, and his face looked like home. "I'm so sorry." She threw herself into his arms, all her carefully laid plans of welcoming him home evaporating into a simple embrace and another whispered apology.

He caught her around the waist, his smile quick and his hug tight. "I love you," he finally said, setting her back onto her feet. The declaration made her feel a bit wobbly.

"I thought maybe if I sold you the farm, you wouldn't be so angry with me for buying it." He stroked his thumb down the side of her face while his other hand worked out the elastic that held her braid captive.

"I was stupid," she said. "I'm not going to take your farm from you. You love this farm."

"I do." He gazed down at her, that sexy smile stuck to his face.

"And I love you too." She stretched up on her toes as he finally got the elastic off the end of her braid and started combing his fingers through her hair. She kissed him, glad he'd come back, beyond relieved she'd been here when he did, grateful for her second chance with him.

———

"Tucker." Ben pushed open the office door. "Oh, sorry," he said when he caught Tucker holding Missy.

"It's fine, Ben." Tucker cleared his throat and stepped in front of Missy so she could hide the blush in her face. Tucker adored that flush, the tenderness in her lips, the easy way she'd apologized and meant it. "Did you get the horses?"

"Two more are out. We could use some additional hands on deck."

"We'll be right out." Tucker waited until Ben closed the door before twisting back to Missy. "Let's go round up some horses." He lifted his arm over her shoulders. "Cowboys do that, right?"

She tipped her head back and laughed, revealing that slender, kissable neck. "I'd really like to see you do that, cowboy."

A month later, Tucker hauled case after case of water from his garage to his truck. The horse show at Steeple Ridge Farm was starting in a couple of hours, and he had a full day ahead of him.

He glanced into the cab of his truck for the tenth time, as if the little black box holding a big, beautiful diamond wouldn't be right where he'd left it. He hadn't sold the farm to Missy, but he was going to give it to her one way or the other. Honestly, he wanted the other, because it meant he got to wake up next to Missy, and go home to Missy, and spoil, spend time with, and share his life with Missy.

"I'll see you out there," he called into the kitchen, where his parents sipped coffee and snacked on the cinnamon rolls Gladys had brought over the previous evening.

His nerves rioted as he pulled into the farm and found Missy's truck already there. He left the water where it was and collected the jewelry box. It seemed to weigh twice as much as all twenty cases of water he'd hauled that morning.

Missy came out of the main barn with Diamond King behind her. "Hey," she said when she saw him. "You're early."

"I could say the same thing to you." He held the box behind his back, his throat so dry he thought it would stick together.

"Wanted to ride for a few minutes."

"Can I ask you something first?"

"Sure."

He collected Diamond's reins from her and dropped to one knee. "Will you marry me?" He swept the diamond out from behind his back, everything happening in less than three seconds.

Missy stared down at him, blinking once, twice before she blurted, "Yes!"

He laughed, leapt to his feet, and twirled her around. With steady hands, he slipped the ring onto her finger, liking the way it looked sitting there. Gazing down at her, he said, "I came to Steeple Ridge to start over." He swallowed, reminding himself that she'd already said yes. "And I want to do that with you. I love you, Missy, and your loud family and your passion for horses, and I even like that old dog of yours that cornered me the first time I came to this farm."

With a beam of happiness in her eyes, she said, "I love you too, Tucker, even if you are a city slicker."

"I'm gonna let that comment slide," he said, his voice lowering to nothing more than a murmur. "After all, I brought in that horse after you missed 'im." He kissed her before she could slap his chest in protest or tease him for his cowboy twang. The way she matched his movement and melted into him sent his happiness soaring.

"I can't wait for you to meet my parents," he whispered as he held her close to his heart. "Then I can introduce you as my fiancée."

She pressed her cheek to his heartbeat. "You wanna ride with me until it's time to set up?"

"'Course." Tucker stepped out of her embrace and went to saddle his horse, his step light as he walked. As he saddled the black stallion, he thanked the Lord that he'd been led to the town of Island Park, to Steeple Ridge Farm, to Missy, and that he'd been given the opportunity to restart his life.

Read on for a sneak peek of **HER RESTLESS COWBOY**, the first full-length novel in the Steeple Ridge Romance series!

Order it in ebook, paperback, or audiobook by scanning the QR code below.

SNEAK PEEK! HER RESTLESS COWBOY - CHAPTER 1

Ben Buttars thundered down the stairs, a bit of dust rising into the air from his boots. Or maybe that was from the wooden stairs that hadn't been swept in a while. The boss hired a maid service that came in twice a month, but once spring thawed and all the mud dried to dirt, not even a daily cleaning could keep the two-story house dust-free.

"Something smells good," his oldest brother, Sam, said as he pushed through the back door and into the kitchen, where Ben had just entered. He snatched a pair of oven mitts from the counter and opened the door to a blast of heat.

Ben flinched away lest he get burned. "Soft pretzels. Your afternoon snack." He grinned, though the memory of his mother always came with the sight and smell of the last snack she'd made for him before she died. Ben had perfected her recipe over the past ten years.

"Mustard?" Sam bent to look in the fridge.

"Already on the counter. Ketchup too." Ben slid the sheet tray onto the stovetop and gazed down at the perfectly browned snack.

"No one eats ketchup on pretzels," Sam said.

"I do." Ben tossed him a grin just as both of their phones sounded. He groaned while Sam simply checked his without any alarm on his face. But Ben was supposed to have the afternoon off before meeting with the recreational director about…something his boss had seemed deliberately dodgy about. And he'd been planning to stuff himself silly with salty pretzels and ketchup.

"Horses out above pasture six," Sam said, lifting his eyes to Ben's. Out of his three brothers, Ben looked the most like Sam—the most like their father, who'd had eyes the color of russet potato skins and hair several shades darker than that. The twins, who sat in between Ben and Sam, had lighter hair and their mother's darker eyes. All four boys had freckles and broad shoulders and a love for the outdoors.

Only Ben had been a minor when their parents had passed away. Only Ben had been forced to leave high school before he'd graduated. Only Ben hadn't dated someone in the last decade.

"Right now?" he asked, and he hated that it sounded more like a whine than a question.

"Right now." Sam started toward the back door, smashing his cowboy hat lower onto his head.

"But the pretzels—"

"They'll keep." Sam's voice filtered back toward him just before the screen door slammed. Frustration threaded through Ben. "They'll keep" was Sam's standard answer for everything.

What should we do with Mom and Dad's stuff?

It'll keep.

Shouldn't we go back to Wyoming? Sell the house?

It'll keep.

Ben cast one last look at the steaming pretzels—which would be ten times better hot—before following his brother out of the house they shared. The blue May sky of Vermont stretched before him, the barns and public parking areas of Steeple Ridge Farm just steps from the house.

The pastures, however, lay to the north and west, in the same direction of the wooded area where Ben liked to let his horse wander after a long day of farm work. He strode toward the back barn, where they housed the farm's horses, including his mare, Willow.

Her dark brown coat glistened, because Ben took immaculate care of her. He'd allow dust in the house, but certainly not on his horse. "All right, girl," he said as he put the saddle on and cinched it. "Let's do this quickly, okay? Because I made pretzels." He led the horse out of the barn and swung onto her back.

Steeple Ridge boarded horses, and the five they had from a barn in northern New York had been nothing but trouble since they'd arrived last week. They seemed to have a knack for finding—or creating—weaknesses in fences and running wild through the woods until they came to the stream.

Bracken ferns grew there, and these New York horses

seemed to have developed a taste for it, though if they ate enough of it they could experience a loss of nerve function. As the manager of the boarding stable, Sam didn't much want to return nerve-damaged horses to the New York clients. With hot pretzels still on his mind, saving the horses from their own fern obsession was a toss-up for Ben.

He joined his brothers and they spread out into the woods, ropes at the ready. The owners of the farm, Tucker and Missy Jenkins, had gone into town to purchase supplies for the upcoming weekend barbecue, or they'd be saddled up and rope-ready too.

Ben whistled as he ducked under a tree branch. A rustling sound to his left drew his attention, and he had one of the New York devil-horses roped a few seconds later. One of them, though, eluded all the brothers until finally Ben couldn't take it anymore.

"How about I take these four back?" he asked Sam, trying to make it sound like he didn't care if he went or not. But he feared that if he didn't go in the next five minutes, he wouldn't even have time to scarf down a single bite of pretzel before his meeting with the recreational director.

He searched his memory for her name but came up blank. While he and his brothers had arrived at Steeple Ridge at the end of last summer, he didn't get into town for much more than church. And even then, he didn't always attend.

There was something soothing and peaceful about the woods, and sometimes the Sabbath simply found him communing with nature, which allowed him to feel closer to God. It had taken him a good five years to accept that God was still loving, still wise and omnipotent, after his parents' plane crash. Sometimes being outside with only trees, birds, and sky reminded him of God's power better than anything a pastor could say.

"Go on, then," Sam said. "Darren, you stay with me. Logan, help 'im get those horses properly secured. Lots of water."

In another situation, Ben might have asked if his brother thought any of the horses had already consumed something poisonous out in the woods, but today, he didn't. He simply set Willow toward the farm and urged her to go a little faster than he would have normally.

"Is there a fire?" Logan asked, coming up beside him.

"I made pretzels," Ben said.

Logan laughed, a big, boisterous sound that filled the sky with noise—and Ben's blood with annoyance. "You and your pretzels."

"I don't see you complaining when you eat them." Ben nudged Willow again and she almost picked up her trot.

"Nope," Logan said. "Never will. I don't know how you get them so stretchy and crispy at the same time. It's amazing."

Some of the tension drained from Ben's shoulders, and he grinned at his next oldest brother.

"Ah, spicy brown mustard," Logan said. "We have some, right?"

"Dunno." Sam did all the grocery shopping for the

brothers. "If you put it on the list at some point, I'm sure we do."

They arrived back on the farm and got the horses brushed down and properly secured in their box stalls. By the time Ben had Willow safe and secure, the very idea of a pretzel had faded to a dot on the horizon. Because he was now late for his appointment.

Sure enough, when he exited the barn, a shiny black sedan sat in the public parking lot. The car looked like it had never been on a farm.

"There you are."

He turned at the feminine voice to find a tall, athletic brunette striding away from the house and toward him. She'd definitely never been on a farm either. Ben drank in the length of her legs, very aware of the pinch of interest in his chest. Her dark brown ponytail swung from side to side, and Ben wondered what her hair would feel like between his fingers.

He swallowed. This woman was so far out of his league, he couldn't even get there in a rocket ship. She paused a healthy distance from him, cocked her hip, and folded her arms. "Which one of you is Ben?"

He glanced at Logan, who wore an expression of half-horror, half-surprise. "He is." Logan hooked his thumb at Ben and walked toward the house. Once he'd passed the beautiful woman, he turned back and beamed for all he was worth, lifting both arms in victory. "I'll save you a pretzel!" he called before turning around and hurrying into the house.

Ben waved at him like it was no big deal, that pretzels

didn't matter at all That river of desire built into something bigger even as he tried to tame it. "I've forgotten your name," he said. "Missy told me, but." He laughed, the sound so full of nerves he wondered how his brothers had ever figured out how to talk to a woman, hold hands with a woman, kiss a woman. Not that they dated all that much, but Sam had had a girlfriend or two, and Logan was definitely a charmer. He could talk to women all day, and Ben had watched him do it, trying to discover the secret. So far, he hadn't figured much out.

His stomach twisted and his mouth went dry dry dry. He'd just forgotten his own name, let alone hers.

"Reagan Cantwell," she said, coming forward again. She extended her hand toward him to shake. He did, trying not to notice the softness of her skin or the strength in her touch. Or the beauty in the lines of her face. Or the depth of her eyes.

She existed on another planet, where men with a lot of money existed. More talent. More brain cells.

"My friends call me Rae."

"Like a ray of sunshine." He smiled but when she didn't, he wiped it from his face quickly, pure foolishness flooding him.

"So Missy tells me you'll have all the info on the horseback riding lessons she wants the rec center to sponsor."

When he stood there, his thoughts stampeding like those crazy New York horses, she lifted her eyebrows as if to say *Well?*

Ben stumbled back a couple of steps. "The horseback

riding lessons. Right. Yes. I know about that." And though he didn't really know what a partnership would look like, he walked forward, drew in a deep breath of her scent and got a noseful of angel food cake and chocolate.

His mouth watered but he still managed to say, "I have all the details in the office in the house. You want to come in?" He'd never been more relieved than when she came with him. And the folder Missy had put on the desk in the office really calmed him. So he hadn't looked at it yet. He could wing this meeting—as long as he didn't look directly at Rae. If he did, he might not even remember how to ride.

Can she figure out how to put what matters most in her life—family and faith—above her job before she loses Ben? Find out in **HER RESTLESS COWBOY**, the next book in the Steeple Ridge Romance series.

Order it in ebook, paperback, or audiobook by scanning the QR code below.

Her Billionaire Cowboy (Book 1): Tucker Jenkins has had enough of tall buildings, traffic, and has traded in his technology firm in New York City for Steeple Ridge Horse Farm in rural Vermont. Missy Marino has worked at the farm since she was a teen, and she's always dreamed of owning it. But her ex-husband left her with a truckload of debt, making her fantasies of owning the farm unfulfilled. Tucker didn't come to the country to find a new wife, but he supposes a woman could help him start over in Steeple Ridge. Will Tucker and Missy be able to navigate the shaky ground between them to find a new beginning?

Her Restless Cowboy: A Butters Brothers Novel, Steeple Ridge Romance (Book 2): Ben Buttars is the youngest of the four Buttars brothers who come to Steeple Ridge Farm, and he finally feels like he's landed somewhere he can make a life for himself. Reagan Cantwell is a decade older than Ben and the recreational direction for the town of Island Park. Though Ben is young, he knows what he wants—and that's Rae. Can she figure out how to put what matters most in her life—family and faith—above her job before she loses Ben?

Her Faithful Cowboy: A Butters Brothers Novel, Steeple Ridge Romance (Book 3): Sam Buttars has spent the last decade making sure he and his brothers stay together. They've been at Steeple Ridge for a while now, but with the youngest married and happy, the siren's call to return to his parents' farm in Wyoming is loud in Sam's ears. He'd just go if it weren't for beautiful Bonnie Sherman, who roped his heart the first time he saw her. Do Sam and Bonnie have the faith to find comfort in each other instead of in the people who've already passed?

Her Mistletoe Cowboy: A Butters Brothers Novel, Steeple Ridge Romance (Book 4): Logan Buttars has always been good-natured and happy-go-lucky. After watching two of his brothers settle down, he recognizes a void in his life he didn't know about. Veterinarian Layla Guyman has appreciated Logan's friendship and easy way with animals when he comes into the clinic to get the service dogs. But with his future at Steeple Ridge in the balance, she's not sure a relationship with him is worth the risk. Can she rely on her faith and employ patience to tame Logan's wild heart?

Her Patient Cowboy: A Butters Brothers Novel, Steeple Ridge Romance (Book 5): Darren Buttars is cool, collected, and quiet—and utterly devastated when his girlfriend of nine months, Farrah Irvine, breaks up with him because he wanted her to ride her horse in a parade. But Farrah doesn't ride anymore, a fact she made very clear to Darren. She returned to her childhood home with so much baggage, she doesn't know where to start with the unpacking. Darren's the only Buttars brother who isn't married, and he wants to make Island Park his permanent home—with Farrah. Can they find their way through the heartache to achieve a happily-ever-after together?

Graham (Book 1): Graham Whittaker returns to Coral Canyon a few days after Christmas—after the death of his father. He takes over the energy company his dad built from the ground up and buys a high-end lodge to live in—only a mile from the home of his once-best friend, Laney McAllister. They were best friends once, but Laney's always entertained feelings for him, and spending so much time with him while they make Christmas memories puts her heart in danger of getting broken again…

Eli (Book 2): Since the death of his wife a few years ago, Eli Whittaker has been running from one job to another, unable to find somewhere for him and his son to settle. Meg Palmer is Stockton's nanny, and she comes with her boss, Eli, to the lodge, her long-time crush on the man no different in Wyoming than it was on the beach. When she confesses her feelings for him and gets nothing in return, she's crushed, embarrassed, and unsure if she can stay in Coral Canyon for Christmas. Then Eli starts to show some feelings for her too…

Andrew (Book 3): Andrew Whittaker is the public face for the Whittaker Brothers' family energy company, and with his older brother's robot about to be announced, he needs a press secretary to help him get everything ready and tour the state to make the announcements. When he's hit by a protest sign being carried by the company's biggest opponent, Rebecca Collings, he learns with a few clicks that she has the background they need. He offers her the job of press secretary when she thought she was going to be arrested, and not only because the spark between them in so hot Andrew can't see straight.

Can Becca and Andrew work together and keep their relationship a secret? Or will hearts break in this classic romance retelling reminiscent of *Two Weeks Notice*?

Beau (Book 4): Beau Whittaker has watched his brothers find love one by one, but every attempt he's made has ended in disaster. Lily Everett has been in the spotlight since childhood and has half a dozen platinum records with her two sisters. She's taking a break from the brutal music industry and hiding out in Wyoming while her ex-husband continues to cause trouble for her. When she hears of Beau Whittaker and what he offers his clients, she wants to meet him. Beau is instantly attracted to Lily, but he tried a relationship with his last client that left a scar that still hasn't healed…

Can Lily use the spirit of Christmas to discover what matters most? Will Beau open his heart to the possibility of love with someone so different from him?

Todd (Book 5): Todd Christopherson has just retired from the professional rodeo circuit and returned to his hometown of Coral Canyon. Problem is, he's got no family there anymore, no land, and no job. Not that he needs a job--he's got plenty of money from his illustrious career riding bulls.

Then Todd gets thrown during a routine horseback ride up the canyon, and his only support as he recovers physically is the beautiful Violet Everett. She's no nurse, but she does the best she can for the handsome cowboy. **Will she lose her heart to the billionaire bull rider? Can Todd trust that God led him to Coral Canyon...and Vi?**

Liam (Book 6): Rose Everett isn't sure what to do with her life now that her country music career is on hold. After all, with both of her sisters in Coral Canyon, and one about to have a baby, they're not making albums anymore.

Liam Murphy has been working for Doctors Without Borders, but he's back in the US now, and looking to start a new clinic in Coral Canyon, where he spent his summers.

When Rose wins a date with Liam in a bachelor auction, their relationship blooms and grows quickly. **Can Liam and Rose find a solution to their problems that doesn't involve one of them leaving Coral Canyon with a broken heart?**

Finn (Book 7): Her sons want her to be happy, but she's too old to be set up on a blind date...isn't she?

Amanda Whittaker has been looking for a second chance at love since the death of her husband several years ago. Finley Barber is a cowboy in every sense of the word. Born and raised on a racehorse farm in Kentucky, he's since moved to Dog Valley and started his own breeding stable for champion horses. He hasn't dated in years, and everything about Amanda makes him nervous.

Will Amanda take the leap of faith required to be with Finn? Or will he become just another boyfriend who doesn't make the cut?

Zach (Book 8): When Celia Abbott-Armstrong runs into a gorgeous cowboy at her best friend's wedding, she decides she's ready to start dating again.

But the cowboy is Zach Zuckerman, and the Zuckermans and Abbotts have been at war for generations.

Can Zach and Celia find a way to reconcile their family's differences so they can have a future together?

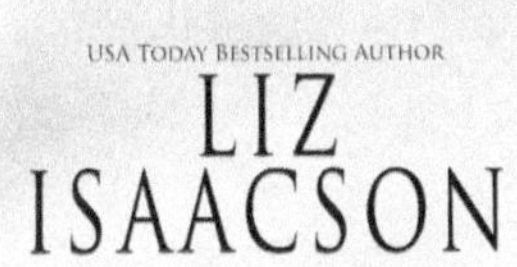

Rhett (Book 1): To save her business, she'll have to risk her heart. She needs a husband to be credible as a matchmaker. He wants to help a neighbor. **Will their fake marriage take them out of the friend zone?**

Tripp (Book 2): She needs a husband to keep her son. He's wanted to take their relationship to the next level, but she's always pushing him away. Will their trivial tie take them all the way to happily-ever-after?

Liam (Book 3): She's desperate to save her ranch. He wants to help her any way he can. Will their invented I-Do open doors that have previously been closed and lead to a happily-ever-after for both of them?

Jeremiah (Book 4): He wants to prove to his brothers that he's not broken. She just wants him. Will a fake marriage heal him or push her further away?

Wyatt (Book 5): To get her inheritance, she needs a husband. He's wanted to fly with her for ages. Can their pretend pledge turn into something real?

Skyler (Book 6): She needs a new last name to stay in school. He's willing to help a fellow student. Can this wanna-be wife show the playboy that some things should be taken seriously?

Micah (Book 7): They were just actors auditioning for a play. The marriage was just for the audition – until a clerical error results in a legal marriage. Can these two ex-lovers negotiate this new ground between them and achieve new roles in each other's lives?

Gideon (Book 8): It's 1971, and Gideon Walker is on the cutting edge of all the technology coming out of Texas. He has big dreams and wants to make something of himself. Then he meets Penny Aarons, and everything changes. He only has eyes for her, but she's got plans and dreams of her own...

Read this origin romance for Momma and Daddy from the Seven Sons series today!

ABOUT LIZ

Liz Isaacson writes inspirational romance, usually set in Texas, or Wyoming, or anywhere else horses and cowboys exist. She lives in Utah, where she writes full-time, takes her two dogs to the park everyday, and eats a lot of veggies while writing. Find her on her website at feelgoodfictionbooks.com